Darkroom

Darkroom

K. R. Alexander

Scholastic Inc.

This book is a work of fiction. Names, characters, places, and incidents are either the product of the author's imagination or are used fictitiously, and any resemblance to actual persons, living or dead, business establishments, events, or locales is entirely coincidental.

ISBN 978-1-338-80733-2

10 9 8 7 6 5 4 3 2 1   22 23 24 25 26

Printed in the U.S.A. 40

First edition, September 2022

Book design by Keirsten Geise

FOR MY ORIGINAL LATE-NIGHT HORROR
GAME CREW—YOU KNOW WHO YOU ARE

O

I never wanted anyone to get hurt.

Really.

If I had known what was going to happen, if I had known the horrors that would be unleashed, I never would have downloaded the game.

I just wanted to find something scary. Something Rochelle and I could stream together, something that would make us laugh and scream out at silly jump scares. And, ideally, something that would get us a few new followers. Something that would make us popular. Something that would prove we weren't just a couple of losers.

Honestly—that's it. I wanted to be popular so I'd stop being the butt of everyone's jokes. Gaming was the only way I could do that.

Which was why, when I found **DARK[room]**, I thought I'd finally found my claim to fame. It was an indie horror game, and the premise was simple: Use your phone to take pictures of—and capture—ghosts.

Easy. Not that many kids had heard about it, it was supposed to be really scary, and I thought it might be the perfect game to get people to check out our channel.

But I was wrong.

I was so, so wrong.

DARK[room] wasn't a game. It was a curse.

Games aren't supposed to be able to hurt you.

You're supposed to be able to turn them off and walk away.

You're supposed to be able to tell yourself that it's okay to be scared—none of it is real.

And most importantly, you're supposed to be able to start over if you die.

But **DARK[room]** ignored all those rules.

Even the last one.

FRIDAY

Day One

1

"Heads up, nerd!" someone calls behind me. Just before a football whizzes past my ear.

I jerk away so fast I nearly crash into a passing junior. She pushes me away with barely a side glance. It's been a month of sophomore year at Montrose High, and I'm still not given more than a glance by anyone.

The hall is packed with my classmates. Everyone talking and laughing, making plans for the weekend even though Friday's only just begun. I overhear the football jocks (the same ones who nearly beaned me with a football) talking about the big game coming up and wonder if it's *actually* a big game or if they just say that about every game because they're on a losing streak. Other kids are talking about parties or gossiping about classmates and teachers. No one talks to me as I pack up my books and homework.

It's fine. I'm used to it.

I just don't *want* to be used to it.

"Hey, Beatrice" comes a familiar voice. I close my locker to see my only real friend, Rochelle. She has her flute case clutched to her chest and a grin on her face. "Still on for tonight?"

Instantly, the frustration fades. Rochelle and I have been friends since fourth grade. She's a little shorter than me, with big dimples and purple-and-rose ribbons woven through her braids, and big, kind eyes. She looks like a Black anime character, especially with her glittery burgundy eye shadow and bright purple lipstick. Even her nails match the color scheme. She's in band and also somehow kinda popular with the cool kids. She works on the school newspaper and volunteers at an animal shelter on the weekends. She's basically Wonder Woman.

She's also a complete game nerd, just like me.

"Heck yeah," I say. "What are we streaming tonight?"

For the last few months, she and I have been trying to build up a following by streaming games online. We only have a few subscribers so far—and they're mostly people we know from various MMOs—and we haven't gotten any donations yet, but the goal is to do it full-time someday. We're definitely good enough, and funny enough. We call ourselves the Ghastly Girls, and we specialize in playing horror games. The scarier, the better.

"Well," she says, leaning against the locker, "I was thinking we could pick up the new *Zombie Rebellion* game? I've got some store credits and I've heard it's really good."

I groan. "Zombies again? The few followers we have will leave if we do another zombie game. We've already streamed, like, four in the last two months. Heck, *I'm* going to leave the channel if we do another one."

Rochelle rolls her eyes. "Do you have any other ideas?"

I don't. I've been trying to think of something—anything—to make us stand out from the pack since we started, and so far I haven't found it. There has to be the perfect game out there—something that hasn't been overdone, and is so scary it will instantly bring in followers. That's part of the trouble with getting subscribers: Some people still think that girl gamers are too weak or squeamish to play really scary horror games. We not only have to find a way to stand out, we have to find a way to prove everyone wrong.

"Maybe we can find an indie," I suggest. "Something no one's heard of before."

"Because *that* will bring them in," Rochelle mumbles. "No one's going to search for a game they haven't heard of."

"Not true. If we market it right, a small indie game can draw a crowd as well as mainstream," I reply.

She looks like she's about to argue, but she either sees my point or hasn't had enough caffeine yet to put up a fight.

"Okayyyy," she relents. "But if we're playing an indie, you're in charge of finding a good one. *And* you're buying the pizza. Just in case the game isn't any good—I want to get something out of my Friday night."

"I always buy the pizza!"

She just laughs as the bell rings. "What can I say? I like free pizza. See you in English?"

I nod, and she makes her way through the crowd of kids toward her first class.

I grab my own books and head to biology. Even though we have a quiz on plant anatomy, all I can think of is what game we're going to play. I just hope I can find something scary enough to shock even me.

If we're going to do this, I want the screams to be real.

✗✗✗

I spend every free moment of the day scrolling through game sites and forums. I bump into at least three different people in the hall and nearly drop my phone every time, but I don't stop. I have to find something by tonight. The trouble is, everything's already been *done.*

Zombie games? Overplayed.

Slashers? Overhyped.

Haunted house games? Completely dull unless they're VR, but I don't have that kind of equipment.

Every time I think I've found something cool, a quick search shows that at least a dozen other streamers have already done it—and some of them have racked up millions of views. I know that it's inevitable, but I don't want to do something someone else has already made famous. I don't want to be a follower. I want to stand out. I want to be known.

"Find anything yet?" Rochelle asks me at lunch.

I jolt and look up.

"How long have you been there?" I ask.

She grins over her tray of food. Now that I'm focused on something other than my phone, I'm back in the loud drone of the cafeteria, my tray of lasagna uneaten and Rochelle looking at me like I've lost it.

"Let's just say your cookies were stale."

I look to my tray. Sure enough, she stole both of my chocolate chip cookies, and I didn't even notice.

"Hey!" I yelp.

"What?" she asks with a giggle. "*You* weren't eating them." Her expression goes serious. "You didn't answer my question: Have you found anything yet? The clock is ticking and *Zombie Rebellion* is only on sale for another two hours."

"Not yet," I say. "But I'm not ready to admit defeat. I will persevere!"

"You are *such* a nerd," she replies.

"Yeah, and you're friends with me, so what does that say about you?"

"That I have really bad taste in friends," she replies without missing a beat. But she's smiling as she says it.

"How about this?" I say. "I've got gym next period. If I don't find anything by the end of it, I'll text you and you can get *Zombie Rebellion*."

I make sure to twist the name of the game, so she gets the full impact of my spite.

"Deal," she says. "But you're still buying me pizza."

"That's not fair. You already stole my cookies."

"And you're making me wait. The anticipation is killing me."

"Then stop interrupting me," I reply.

"Good luck, Sherlock. Don't let me interfere." She grabs my garlic bread, takes a bite, and tosses it back on my tray. "The clock is ticking . . ."

2

I tell the gym teacher that I don't feel well, and he lets me sit it out. I perch up in the bleachers, away from the other fakers, and keep my phone hidden in my rolled-up hoodie, pretending to watch the rest of my class play volleyball while I scroll.

And really, I'm not faking—my head hurts from all the staring and scrolling, from trying to find anything remotely unique and interesting. I start to worry that maybe Rochelle is right—maybe we're just doomed to stream the same things as everyone else. She doesn't seem to understand why it's so important to me that we stand out. She doesn't get why we *have* to be unique.

She's already popular. She already has more than one friend. She doesn't get made fun of.

"I hear she doesn't shower, like, ever," a voice in front of me says.

I try to tune it out.

I found a thread about banned video games, and I

think I might be onto something. There's a lot of creepy stuff on here. But most of it is too gory or gross. I don't want to get banned from streaming. I just want to find something scary.

"Not like it matters," says another voice. "No one is ever around her."

"Just that suck-up," the first girl says. "Ugh, did you hear that they've started filming themselves playing video games? How stupid is that?"

Sweat breaks out over my skin, but still I focus on my phone. I look up and see it's Claire and Kaitlin, two cheerleaders who have had it out for me since fifth grade, now sitting a few rows in front of me. I try to tune them out. It doesn't work.

"Oh my gosh, right?" Kaitlin says. "Who would even want to watch that? I'd rather poke out my eyes."

"Well," Claire says with a harsh giggle, "at least then you wouldn't have to see her!"

I can't take it anymore. My chest hurts and my throat is tight and I can't read the thread because my eyes are blurry.

"No wonder she isn't dating anyone," Kaitlin continues. "I mean, who would want to go out with *her*?"

I look up.

Claire and Kaitlin are looking at me, not even trying to pretend they're talking about someone else. Rather than look away embarrassed, they immediately burst into giggles. Claire is white with short blonde hair, and Kaitlin is Filipino, her dark hair pulled up in a bun. Both of them are cheerleaders, which means both of them think they're better than me. The worst part is, sometimes, I let myself think they're right.

I glare at them, but I don't hold it for long. There's no point.

I wipe my eyes and return to my reading. The title of the thread I'm on now is pretty clear.

DON'T PLAY THIS GAME

Ugh, what horrible advertising, I think. But I click the thread anyway and start to read.

I REPEAT. DO NOT PLAY THIS GAME. I KNOW THIS SOUNDS LIKE A JOKE BUT I BEG YOU PLEASE DO NOT PLAY THIS GAME. MY FRIEND STARTED PLAYING IT LAST WEEK AND NOW HE IS DEAD. HE SAID HE SAW GHOSTS AND THINGS AND THEN THEY GOT HIM. PLEASE PLEASE PLEASE DON'T PLAY THIS GAME.

—concerned user

What game? Dude you can't leave us hanging.

—*gamergeek723*

Yeah man. What are you talking about? This sounds sick.

—*anonymouse7*

We can't avoid it if we don't know what it is!

—*logical1*

IT'S CALLED "DARK[room]" BUT PLEASE PLEASE DON'T PLAY IT. I DIDN'T WANT TO SHARE THE NAME BECAUSE I DON'T WANT PEOPLE SEARCHING FOR IT. BUT YOU HAVE TO AVOID IT. PLEASE. SAVE YOURSELF.

—*concerned user*

No worries there man. I can't find it anywhere.

—*gamergeek723*

Yeah is it unlisted or something?

—*logical1*

Wait wait I found it. You have to email them? That's stupid.
I don't like giving out my info.

—*gamergeek723*

DON'T DO IT PLEASE. YOU WILL DIE. DON'T LET THEM IN.

—concerned user

Hah, nice try OP.
Got the invite. Can't wait to play. Gonna start tonight. Full moon wooo spoopy.

—anonymouse7

Where?! I wanna play!

—logical1

Easy. Just email [LINK] and they'll send you a download link.

—anonymouse7

NO! DON'T DO IT!

—concerned user

This game is SICK. So scary. That crawling woman gives me nightmares. Link attached.

—anonymouse7

Heck yeah! Got it, too. They only give you a twelve-hour window to respond and download so gonna start tonight. Can't wait!

—logical1

> **NO!**
> —*concerned user*

> **It's been a few days. What do you guys think?**
> **Worth it?**
> —*gamergeek723*

> **Guys? Status update?**
> —*gamergeek723*

> **Hellooooo?**
> —*gamergeek723*

> **Fine. Guess I'll download.**
> —*gamergeek723*

> **PLEASE IF YOU READ THIS DON'T DOWNLOAD.**
> **THEY'RE DEAD. THEY'RE ALL DEAD. AND SHE'S**
> **COMING AFTER ME**
> —*gamergeek723*

My fingers shake as I get to the bottom of the thread.

I scroll back up. Check the dates.

These were posted only a few weeks ago. How have I not heard about this game? The creators of **DARK[room]** are clearly trying to go for the crowd-sourced, word-of-mouth sort of advertising. I mean, creating an entire thread warning people away? Not a bad idea—nothing gets people to do something like telling them *not* to do it.

I figure if I email them and tell them I'm a streamer, they'll let me play. Maybe the creators will even help promote me if I say I'm just starting out. We could help each other.

This could be perfect.

I scroll to the email and click the hyperlink.

My email app pops up, a blank message drafted to the game's creators. At least, I hope it's them. I hate giving out my info online, too, but that's why Rochelle and I created a whole set of contact details specifically for the Ghastly Girls.

I type out a quick email.

I saw the thread warning people away from DARK[room].
Awesome idea.

My friend and I are streamers specializing in scary games.
We'd love to play. And maybe collab?

I don't hit send, though.

Something makes me pause.

What if it *wasn't* a marketing scheme?

What if these really were normal gamers, and something horrible actually happened to them?

I consider deleting the message.

Then I hear Kaitlin and Claire burst into laughter. And when I look at them, it's clear they're looking at me. I don't know what they've said, but I know it isn't flattering.

I hit send. Right as someone yells my name.

3

I'm in big trouble.

If I'd thought that Coach Vaughn giving me detention and taking away my phone was bad, the disappointment in my parents' eyes when I get home is even worse. As is their verdict:

"No phone or games all weekend," my mom says. She paces back and forth in front of me while my dad just shakes his head. I can practically hear him saying, *We raised you better.* Probably because he's already said it a dozen times.

"But, Mom—"

"No *buts*!" she interrupts. *Ugh.* I haven't managed to get a word in this entire fight. I'd barely taken a full step into the doorway before they laid into me. "You know the rules—no phones at school. A phone is a *privilege*, not a right. And since you have gone ahead and flouted the rules, that privilege is being taken away."

"But I'm supposed to stream tonight!" I say in a rush.

"We said no games," Dad answers.

"But it's not playing games!"

Mom scoffs. "You and Rochelle get together and, what? You aren't doing homework on that computer, I know that much."

"We're building a *career*," I insist.

It's no use, though; they've never understood.

When I first told them I wanted to get into streaming, the first question was, *Why?* and the next was, *Is it dangerous?* Dad practically flipped when he learned Rochelle and I were going to be filming ourselves playing games and putting it online.

You don't know the type of people who are out there, he'd warned.

It had taken months—months!—to convince them to let us stream. And only *after* Dad had sat in on our first stream (which was beyond awkward, let me tell you) and given it the okay.

Now it looks like all that effort is coming to nothing.

"Playing. Games. Is. Not. A. Career," my mother snips. I swear, she looks like she's about to pop.

I don't see why they're so upset. I've only ever gotten a detention once before, and that was for missing three assignments in a row . . . and, *yes*, that was because I'd been getting our streaming gear set up, but it wasn't a big deal!

"It *is* a career!" I reply. "There are people who make, like, six figures a *month* doing it. And a lot of them aren't much older than me."

"And how much have *you* gotten paid, Beatrice?" Dad asks.

His words are a stab to the heart.

I look to my feet.

"Nothing."

Five months of streaming, and we still didn't have a single paid subscriber or donation.

"Precisely," he said. "Which means it's *not* a job. *School* is your job right now, and your mother and I expect you to be applying yourself to that job *full-time*."

"But—"

"No," Mom says. "You were caught using your phone in class. Looking up video games, no doubt. And I know that Rochelle is a sweet girl, but she's just helped overexcite you about this whole streaming thing. Your father is right: School needs to be your priority."

I open my mouth . . . but what can I say?

Mom notes my silence and continues. "Now, go to your room. And, Frank, make sure you get her laptop, too. And her tablet. Ugh, you kids have more devices than a picnic has ants . . ."

She stomps off toward the kitchen, leaving Dad and me alone in the living room.

"*Dad*," I whine.

"Don't *Dad* me," he replies. "You should just be thankful we aren't getting rid of all your equipment."

My stomach lurches.

My streaming equipment. I've spent *hundreds* on decent microphones and cameras and headphones. All from my carefully saved babysitting and lawn-mowing money. It took over a year to save up for it. He can't really be suggesting they'll just throw it all away?

When I look at his stormy expression, however, I realize he would most *definitely* toss it all away.

I swallow my response and follow him upstairs to my bedroom where—sure enough—he grabs my laptop and tablet and turns to go.

He pauses to look at me. I sit on my bed, not speaking, not looking at anything but my feet. It feels like he's taking a part of me away, and all I can think is: *It's not fair.*

I was so close to finding something that could really make me famous. Could really make this a career, and could make those jerks stop making fun of me.

If you're famous, no one can make fun of you. Or at least, if you're famous, you don't have to hear it.

"This is for your own good," Dad says. "I know it doesn't feel like it now, but it is. I swear."

Then he leaves.

When I hear his feet disappear back down the steps, I growl a yell and throw a pillow at the door.

"I hate you," I seethe.

4

I know that Rochelle isn't going to come rescue me from my prison.

We'd chatted right before leaving school. She knew that I had gotten in trouble with Coach Vaughn, knew that my cell phone had been taken away in school. She knew that my parents would probably be upset.

I had warned her that they might go volcanic and that if she didn't hear from me by six, streaming was going to be off.

Since, according to my alarm clock, it's already seven, she must know that things aren't looking good. She just has no idea how bad they actually are.

My parents refused to eat dinner with me. I'm grounded to my room for the rest of the night, which meant Dad brought me up a plate of tacos and left it on my bare desk without a word. Like he was a prison guard delivering an inmate's meal. And that's what it feels like. I even feel guilty getting up and going to the bathroom. Well, maybe *guilty* isn't the right word: I feel like even that is enough to get me in further trouble, and every time I open the door, I worry I'll hear the crash and slam of my parents throwing out all my streaming gear.

There's nothing to do except sit at my window and stare out at the clear night. I feel like a creep as I watch people walking their dogs and kids playing in the street, but at least it's something to do. I mean, yeah, I have shelves of books I haven't touched, but I don't want to read. I want to pace and scream because *this isn't fair.* So, I watch everyone else going about their blissful lives and wish I was one of them. None of *them* are grounded because their parents don't understand them or their passions or their dreams. None of *them* have had everything important taken away in the blink of an eye.

But it's not just the unfairness. It's the unknown.

Every few minutes I reach for my phone in my pocket only to remember it isn't there. Or I make to get up from my seat and open my laptop before catching myself.

Because every few minutes, the thought stabs my mind: What if the creators of **DARK[room]** got back to me?

What if there's a time-sensitive email just waiting in my in-box?

What if the answer to all my problems is sitting there, unseen, expiring, and because of my parents, that one opportunity is going to slip through my fingers? The kids on the forum said you only had twelve hours to respond to the game invite before it expired. If I don't act soon, I could miss my chance.

I want to text Rochelle to tell her to check the email account, but of course I can't do that. And since she lives a few miles away, I can't expect her to just walk past on the street so I can call out to her. Maybe that's another reason I don't move from my perch: Just in case. Just in case she's concerned. Just in case she decides to make an hour-long casual stroll past my window.

I know she won't check the email on her own. She's only interested in streaming for the fun factor. Setting up the accounts and researching the best microphones and studying trends—all that falls on me. But at least she's enthusiastic. At least she understands that this could be a real, life-changing career.

Unlike my parents.

They don't understand.

They never will.

It feels like weeks pass as I sit there, watching the night blacken, watching the streets clear until it's just the occasional car driving past. With every passing moment, my anger and frustration grow.

My parents always tell me I should be thinking of my future. Always tell me I shouldn't have my head in the clouds. Which means they don't think I can make it as a streamer. They don't have faith in me or my abilities.

They think I'm a loser.

Just like Claire and Kaitlin and every other kid in my high school who treats me like a loser.

My parents are no better than the worst of them.

No, my parents *are* the worst of them. Because my parents are actively trying to prevent me from following my dreams. They want to see me fail. Just like the popular kids.

Well, I'm not going to let them win. I won't. Ever.

By the time I hear my parents go to bed, I'm so worked up I can't sit still. I've spent the last hour sitting on my bed trying to stay completely silent, the lights off so they think I'm asleep.

I'm not going to let them get away with this. I'm not going to let them ruin my future.

I wait an hour.

Every second ticks by like a scratch on my skin.

And then, when I know it's safe, I slowly, silently open my door.

There's only one place they'd hide my electronics: the library. Which is really just their fancy way of saying the room with some bookshelves and desks where they sometimes work from home.

I sneak down the steps. And maybe it's my

imagination because I know I'm doing something wrong, but I swear the darkness grows heavier with every step down. A cold creeps over my limbs that has nothing to do with the autumn air.

It feels like I'm being watched.

I keep pausing and crouching to look over my shoulder.

I'm so convinced that someone is perched at the top of the stairs, watching me.

Waiting.

Expecting me to mess up.

But my parents aren't up there, and I don't see anyone looking in through the windows.

I'm alone.

That makes it worse.

I almost creep myself out and turn back around. I could still go to bed and forget all this—

No.

I'll sneak in. Get my phone. Check messages. And maybe play a little bit if I got the invite. Just a bit.

Then I'll return my phone and go back to bed and no one will be any wiser. I'll secure the game for our future streaming. I'm not breaking the rules. Just . . . bending them.

The library is quiet. Cold. Dusty and eerie as a mausoleum.

Staying low, I make my way to my dad's desk. My hands pause when I reach for the drawer.

Am I really going to do this? Am I really going to become the person they already think I am by betraying their trust?

I swallow.

I have to do this. For my future. For the stream.

I have to prove to everyone that I'm not someone who's going to be ignored.

I slide open the drawer, and sure enough, my tablet and laptop and phone are right on top. I grab my phone.

I have a bunch of messages—most from Rochelle—but those aren't what make my heart race.

One new email in my streaming account.

There's only, like, 2 percent battery, but I quickly pull up the app, nervously waiting for it to load, my foot tapping impatiently.

It's a response from the **DARK[room]** team. The subject is ominous.

DON'T OPEN THIS EMAIL

I open it.

The rest of the email is just as creepy.

You want to play? You want to be scared? You want to stare into the face of fear?

Grab your phone. DARK[room] awaits.

But beware: Once you release the ghosts, there's no putting them back. Not until you've beaten the game. You only have one week before they destroy you.

You don't want to play this game. It will play back. And it will win.

Still dare to try?

<u>CLICK HERE.</u>

I swallow. The feeling of being watched is even more intense. I swear there are a dozen people standing behind me, breathing down my neck, awaiting my decision.

I hesitate. But only for a moment.

I click the link.

The app downloads in a blink.

And—with a glance around—I click the new game icon: a simple black-and-white old-fashioned camera.

A screen flashes on my phone. Black creepy text, grainy gray background.

WE WARNED YOU

My phone vibrates wildly and goes dead.

5

I nearly drop my phone from the shock. I don't know if it's fear from the warning message or the surprise vibration or the fact that it ran out of juice the moment the game loaded.

I glance around in the pitch darkness, worried my parents heard. My ears throb with my pulse as I listen for their angry steps on the stairs.

But the seconds tick by.

The cold deepens.

The darkness grows heavy.

My parents don't come down.

I know, then, that I have a choice: I've accepted my spot, I've gotten the game. I'm set. I can put the phone back and go back upstairs and be a good girl and wait out the weekend of being grounded.

Or.

Or . . .

Or I can head down to the basement where my streaming gear is set up. I can charge my phone and maybe, just maybe, I can play a little bit of the game.

Maybe, just maybe, I'll even stream it.

I don't know how long I crouch there, chewing my lip and holding my phone to my chest like a baby bird. If I'm quick, my parents won't even know I went down there. It's not like they watch or are subscribed to my stream in the first place—I guess there is a small silver lining to them not taking it seriously. But if I'm caught down there, if my dad comes down for a late-night snack or my mom has insomnia again, I'm in trouble. It's a huge risk.

But then I think of the mean things those girls had said about me. I think about the thrill I'd felt when the game downloaded and—for one brief moment—I'd felt special. I was on the inside.

I'm not ready to let that feeling go. Not just yet. Besides, how killer would it be to show up on Monday an overnight legend? That would make them all see me.

As quietly as I can, I make my way toward the basement.

It's a finished basement, so it looks just like a normal, carpeted living room, except there aren't any windows and it's a lot colder than the rest of the house. There are giant fake plants in the corners, except for the corner I've made my own.

Rochelle and I set up a few desks and monitors

and ring lights, as well as microphones, well-angled cameras, and squishy chairs so we can be comfortable while we play. There's a mini-fridge within arm's reach, so we don't have to go upstairs for pop or snacks. While the rest of the room is beige and boring, our corner is draped in black fabric and plastic bats and purple twinkle lights. We're going with a theme, after all.

I flip all the overhead lights off, leaving just the purple lights draped above me. Less chance my parents will notice this light through the crack of the basement door. At least, I hope so. I'm grateful Rochelle and I invested in the lower-light cameras.

I plug my phone into my rapid charger and wait a few minutes, tapping my foot anxiously. I'm starting to feel the need to pee, but if I get up now there's no way I can come back down here. But it's not just that, or the fear of discovery, that has me on edge.

No.

Ever since my phone died, the feeling of being watched has intensified.

I know I'm down here alone.

I know my back faces a wall and I'd see anything in the room.

But I keep glancing behind me. I keep peering into the shadows just beyond the twinkling lights.

I'm not usually the type who is able to scare themselves—I know when it's just my imagination playing tricks—but at this moment . . .

At this moment I'm not one hundred percent certain that I *am* just scaring myself.

What had the app said? *Once you release the ghosts, there's no putting them back.*

I swear something shifts in the corner of my vision. I glance over.

Was that a pale face hanging upside down from the ceiling?

No, no, it was just a lamp. Just a lamp.

I force myself to laugh.

"Wow," I whisper. Even hearing my own voice is somewhat calming in that unsettling, quiet dark. "You really are letting this get under your skin. It's just a game, Bea. Just a stupid indie video game."

My phone buzzes and I nearly drop it.

It's just turning on.

This time, when I laugh, it's real. My heart hammers in my chest.

Okay, maybe if the game has me this spooked already, it's a winner.

After what feels like forever, my phone fully reboots.

"Okay, then," I say to myself. "Let's get started."

I turn on my computer and flick on the monitors. I quietly test the microphones (and am grateful I took Rochelle's advice and got the high-sensitivity setup that ASMR artists use—not that we usually need it, since we're laughing and screaming) and wave at the cameras to make sure they're on. I put on my headphones and fix my hair and wish I'd put on makeup, before I realize it wouldn't show up anyway in the low light.

Then I pull up the streaming software, log into my account so I can livestream this for the zero people following me, and begin to record.

"Hey, ghosts and ghouls," I whisper. I still cringe at this opener, but Rochelle insisted on it, too. "It's Crimson here, gearing up for a brand-new game installment." (I was the one who insisted on code names for the stream. Mostly because my dad nearly exploded when I first set the stream up under our real names.) "Sorry for the quiet treatment, but I'm technically grounded and I don't want to wake up my parents. If you happen to be watching, sorry, Mom and Dad!

"As you can see, I'm streaming alone tonight because of the grounding, but I just couldn't wait. Hopefully Butterfly doesn't mind too much." (I don't know why she chose that as her name, since we were supposed to be scary, but whatever. I suppose it fits her.) "Tonight, I have something totally new and totally exclusive." I flip my phone around and hold it up to the camera, showing **DARK[room]**'s home screen. "That's right! I have access to an invite-only, just-released game. It's called **DARK[room]**, and there isn't that much information out there on it. It doesn't even have an official website!"

I position one of the cameras so it can track my phone screen while the other records my face, a side-by-side display.

"From what I've read online, it's supposed to be super terrifying. But I have no idea what exactly it is. So! Let's find out and play, shall we?"

The game's home screen is a grainy black-and-white crackle, like static on an old TV screen. There's only one button.

BEGIN

I tap it.

The phone vibrates and switches to camera mode, everything in gray scale.

"Okay," I whisper. "That's strange. Did it glitch?"

But before I can exit the app, words scrawl across the bottom of the screen. I read them aloud as they appear.

SEVEN SPIRITS HAVE BEEN RELEASED.
IT'S UP TO YOU TO PUT THEM BACK.
YOU CANNOT HURT THEM.
YOU CANNOT HIDE FROM THEM.
YOU CAN ONLY PHOTOGRAPH THEM
AND TRAP THEIR SOULS IN YOUR PHONE.

"Huh," I say. "That's a fun premise. Augmented reality in a horror game." But the words don't stop. The next sentences make goose bumps break over my skin.

YOUR TIME IS TICKING. THE GHOSTS ARE HUNGRY.
THEY DON'T GO AWAY WHEN YOU CLOSE THE APP.
THEY DON'T GO TO SLEEP.
THE LONGER YOU WAIT,
THE HUNGRIER THEY GET.
YOU HAVE UNTIL MIDNIGHT ON THE SEVENTH DAY.
THEN YOU WILL JOIN THEM.

DAY ONE STARTS NOW.
GOOD LUCK.

6

"Creepy," I say.

I move the phone around a little bit, taking in the wall in front of me but not wanting to move it too far, in case it moves out of camera. The image on the screen is fuzzy and monochrome. The shadows are ink black, the walls bone white.

"So I just have to take pictures of ghosts? Sounds easy enough. Only seven days though . . . Whatever, I'll beat this way before then. Indie games like this are always pretty short. Especially the free ones."

I'm mostly talking to fill the silence, because nothing is happening onscreen anymore and footage of someone's camera in a boring basement is far from entertaining. The other part of me is talking because the silence feels oppressive. But that's probably just the noise-canceling headphones.

My heart sinks a little. What if the game *is* a dud? What if it isn't scary at all?

Then I hear something.

It must be coming from the game: a low, gravelly moan. Quiet. On my right.

The chills on my arms intensify.

"Do you guys hear that?" I whisper. "I think we have our first ghost."

Making sure I keep the phone screen in view of the cameras, I pivot it around the basement. Looking into the shadows. Although, if I'm honest, the last thing I want to *do* is look into the shadows. Only an idiot wants to *see* a ghost—normal people try to hide.

Instead I sit there like a target.

Trying to find the source of the noise that gets louder

and louder.

Closer

and closer.

"It's close," I say breathlessly. My heart is hammering, and even though I'm starting to sweat, the basement is as frigid as an icy pool. "Come on, where are you?"

That's when I feel it.

I swear I feel it.

Two hands on my ankles.

I point the camera down.

And there,

crawling on the floor by my feet,

is a transparent woman.

Her skin is pale blue onscreen, and the phone vibrates wildly the moment she's in the frame.

She slowly tilts her head back to look at me.

The gravelly moan gets louder.

The feeling of her hands on my ankles grows tighter.

She looks at me.

She has no eyes.

Just black, empty sockets.

She opens her mouth.

Her jaw cracks wide.

Her throat is black, cavernous.

The moan becomes a hungry roar.

Onscreen, a tiny blip appears above her face:

DEVOURING WOMAN

And that's when I remember what I'm supposed to do.

With shaking fingers, I take a picture.

The camera's flash goes off, blinding me in the darkness.

The roar becomes a scream.

The pressure on my ankles vanishes.

When I can see again, the screen is empty. It just shows my feet.

I flop back in my chair and take a deep breath. Press a hand to my heart.

"Whew," I say. "I don't know about you, but I found that to be pretty scary. Can you hear my heart racing? And okay, I know it's stupid and probably just the headphones, but I swear I felt her grabbing my ankles."

I let out a nervous laugh.

Something thuds above me. Footsteps.

I pull off a side of my headphones and listen. Oh no. I think my dad is up.

I drop back to a whisper and lean in to the camera.

"I think I'm gonna need some backup before I go any further. So, on that note, Crimson is signing off. Sweet nightmares."

I stop recording the stream, pull down my headphones, and hope my dad doesn't hear me.

Definitely my dad's footsteps—I'd recognize their sound anywhere.

Please please please don't come down here.

He doesn't.

When I hear him plod back upstairs, I let out a sigh of relief.

I count to a hundred.

Then I switch off all the computer gear and creep upstairs.

It's only when I'm back in the library, quietly slipping my phone back into Dad's desk so we can pretend that I never broke the rules, that I actually look at the screen.

The game is still running, even though I swear I turned it off.

The camera is still up.

But now, there are two words at the bottom. They fade the moment I see them.

YOU MISSED

7

I swear I'm not a jumpy person.

I mean, it was *my* idea to stream horror games in the first place. Rochelle enjoys playing, but she's happy gaming anything so long as she gets to bash things onscreen. It's me who likes horror movies and games and memes. It's me who stays up late reading horror novels. *I'm* the one who has no problem sleeping after watching or reading terrifying tales.

Which is why, when I get upstairs, I'm more surprised at *how* scared I am, rather than actually *being* scared.

What I mean is, I turn on every light in the bathroom when I go in, even though the sudden brightness is blinding. I peer behind the shower curtain. And when I leave, I wait until my eyes adjust to the near-darkness before stepping out into the hall. From there, I run. As silently and softly as I can.

I turn on all the lights in my bedroom.

I check under the bed.

I check in my closet.

I even pull back my drapes to make sure there's nothing hiding behind them.

And when I'm absolutely, *positively* sure that my room is ghost-free, I pull out a night-light from the bottom drawer of my nightstand and plug it in. Even though there isn't anyone around, my cheeks still flush from embarrassment.

I haven't used the thing since I was, like, five. I don't know why I kept it, but right now I'm glad that I did.

Even with its soft glow, my room doesn't feel safe when I turn off the light.

I pull the sheets up over my head and peer out through a crack in the folds.

I watch the shadows occasionally flip as a car goes past.

I scarcely breathe.

And when I close my eyes and swear I feel someone pressing down on my covers, I tell myself it's just my imagination.

There is no ghost in my room.

There is no one perched at the foot of my bed.

Even if I hear them breathing.

It's just a game.

It's just in my head.

It's just a game.

It's just a game . . .

SATURDAY
Day Two

8

"Oh. My. Glob," Rochelle says.

It's Saturday afternoon. I hadn't expected her to come over to my house. My parents were also surprised—so surprised they said she could stay, but only for half an hour. Outside. With no devices.

Rochelle has a way with adults. I think it's the dimples.

"What?" I ask her once we're alone.

"I can't believe you started playing without me!" she yelps.

"Shh!" I hiss.

She looks around, but there isn't anyone out in the front yard with us. The street is empty, and my parents aren't listening in. But I still don't want to risk them hearing that I broke the rules.

"Okay, okay," she says, lowering her voice. "But, seriously? Why didn't you text me or something?"

"I was grounded! No devices, remember?"

She raises an eyebrow. "I mean last night. You

know. When you *had* your phone. Illegally. What, you can play a game without me, but you can't let me know you're okay? I sent you, like, a million texts."

"I'm sorry," I reply. "I didn't even check my messages. I was just . . . I don't know. Focused."

"Mmm-hmmmm," she mumbles. She stands there, arms crossed under her chest, tapping her foot in the perfect imitation of *agitated*. Then her serious face breaks out into a smile. "So, tell me! How was it?"

"It was kinda scary," I reply, trying to play it cool and still failing. I take a few steps toward the sidewalk, just in case my parents are trying to listen in or read our lips through the window. "Didn't you see the ghost?"

"Not really. You kinda jolted and the camera shifted away. You must have knocked the camera. All we saw was you staring under your desk and quivering."

"I wasn't quivering."

"You were. Your teeth were practically chattering. What did you see? What did it look like?"

"It was . . ." I trail off, but not because I can't remember. It's because I can remember it all too well.

Every dream I had last night had the Devouring Woman. Following me down the hall, her mouth gaping and growling, her blank eyes piercing my soul.

46

Her arms scrambling toward me, trying to drag me into her hungry mouth.

Every time she grabbed me, I woke up in a cold sweat.

I could swear she was still there, invisible, crouching on my ankles.

They don't go away when you close the app. That's what the game had said. And I knew it was just marketing, knew it was just a stupid game.

But it still got under my skin.

I barely slept. And even then, only when I had turned on all the lights.

I don't tell Rochelle that. Of course I don't tell her that. I can't let her think I'm losing my nerve to a stupid game. I'd never hear the end of it.

"Well?" she asks, poking me in the ribs.

"It was just a generic ghost lady," I say. I shrug. "Creepy. No eyes. Big mouth. The game said she was called *Devouring Woman.*"

"Oooh, I wonder if she'll try to eat you," Rochelle replies. "Did you capture her?"

I shake my head. "I think I was too slow. You probably have to time it just right and get the ghost perfectly in frame."

At least that's what I'm telling myself. It's not like the game came with detailed instructions. I'm just basing it off similar titles I've played. And, well, trying to convince myself that that's where I went wrong.

Because if it's just a matter of skill, I can get better.

If it's actually impossible to catch the ghosts, however . . .

I shake myself. Here I am, acting like the game is real. Like I have to capture the ghosts Or Else.

It's just. A. Game.

One that gave me bad nightmares.

My dad knocks on the front window. I jolt and look over. He points to his wrist in a clear *time's up* gesture.

"Ugh, gotta go," I say.

"Wait," Rochelle says. She drops her voice to a whisper. "Are you going to stream again tonight?"

"I . . ." I look over my shoulder. Dad's gone from the window, but I still lower my voice. "I'm not certain. I think so. If I do, I'll aim for eleven. They'll be asleep by then."

"Well," she says, breaking into a smile, "it sounds like you better! If that game's telling the truth, you still have a Devouring Woman creeping around your house!"

She giggles.

In the pit of my stomach, I wonder if she's right.

9

I spend the rest of the day not focusing on homework.

I sit in the living room while my parents work and clean around me. It's clearly not going over well.

"Are you sure you don't just want to work in your bedroom?" my mom asks, wiping the counter beside me and shuffling a pile of biology papers to the side. "You *do* have a desk up there, you know."

"I know," I say. "Just needed a change of scenery."

Mom raises an eyebrow at me, but she doesn't push it. At least when I'm down here, she can make sure I'm not sneaking in any screen time.

The truth is, though, I don't really feel safe in my room.

When I was up there getting my homework, I felt a chill, the same sort that I felt in the basement.

I felt like I was being watched.

I hurried back down to the living room as soon as I could.

Being around other people helps me feel less vulnerable.

The strange part is, though, the feeling doesn't make me want to stop playing **DARK[room]**. If anything, it makes me want to play more.

Because if it's scaring *me* this much, and I'm only on the first ghost, there's a great chance it will scare my audience, too.

I just need to not freak myself out too much before we can reach stardom.

×✗×

My parents go to bed around ten.

Even though it freaks me out, I sit on my bed with all the lights off, fully clothed and ready to go, waiting for them to fall asleep. I have a flashlight clutched between my hands, and every once in a while I blink it on to search around the room.

Nothing is there.

Nothing is ever there.

Every time I turn off the light, I shiver nervously and feel the thrill of excitement that always tinges my fear.

I am so scared already, and I've only played the game for two minutes.

I can't wait to bring Rochelle in.

She is going to *scream.*

Finally, when it's nearly eleven, I slip out of my room and make my way to the library.

My phone is right where I left it. The battery is dead—I wonder if the app just constantly runs in the background, which is what it meant by *the ghosts don't sleep.* In any case, I'm glad I have my flashlight, because it's cold and dark and the wind is blowing outside, making branches scratch at the windows like skeletal fingers.

When I make it down to the basement, everything is dead silent. It's like I've stepped into another world.

A very dark, very cold, very oppressive world.

I pause at the top of the basement steps and give the basement a once-over with the flashlight.

Nothing.

All clear.

With the lights still off, I head down the steps and—as a stupid precaution—peer into each of the closets and even the laundry room. But even those dark, creepy places are empty.

I am completely alone down here.

I tell myself this over and over: *I am alone. There are no ghosts. I'm just playing a video game. I am being ridiculous.*

There is nothing scary down here besides what's happening inside my head and on the screen.

Normally, that would be enough to kick me out of a fear spiral. This time, however, the words are far from reassuring. They feel like lies.

Once more, I plug in the phone, turn on the computer, and set up my gear as I wait for it to get a charge. As I wait, I pull up the statistics about last night's stream.

"No way," I gasp.

There are a few notifications at the top.

Not only did the stream attract a dozen new viewers, but they've all subscribed. A few even left comments—mostly about the bad camera angle—but still! People are watching!

> So cool you're playing. I heard about this game but am too chicken to start.

> Can't wait for the nxt. Bring on teh ghosties!

And, no way!

Someone has actually *donated*!

I pull up my messenger on the computer and shoot off a quick message to Rochelle.

> Did you see this? We got PAID!

Her response is immediate.

> YEAH, GIRLIE! Now, get to screaming and give these viewers what they want.

> I meant streaming. Totally meant streaming.

I chuckle. Just then, my phone buzzes and turns on. The moment it's loaded, the **DARK[room]** app opens on its own.

I quickly log in and start the stream, triple-checking that you can see the phone screen from every possible angle.

"Hey, ghosts and ghouls," I whisper. "Crimson here again. Still grounded, still flying solo. But I'm back with another installment of what will definitely be our next Let's Play. Hopefully soon with Butterfly riding shotgun. Every night, until we've gotten this beat. To all our new viewers, welcome. And to our steadfast fans, thanks for dropping back in. And to our donor, a *huge* thank-you."

According to my streaming home page, we have three viewers already logged on. One of them is Rochelle, but still. It's rare we actually stream to an audience. Normally our viewers watch the uploads after the fact.

I hold up the phone, showing the screen.

"As you can see, **DARK[room]** is ready to go. I didn't even log on, it just seems to be constantly running in the background. I think it wants to play." I smile wickedly. "Well, I've been waiting all day for this. Let's capture some ghosts."

10

I quickly realize the problem with my plan.

DARK[room] wants you to explore. That's pretty obvious. It wants you to look in the dark corners and closets and stare into the shadows. I mean, that's the best part of augmented reality—that overlap between tech and the world around you.

Trouble is, having to stay in the computer seat means I can't really explore. All I can do is pivot in my chair and point the flashlight and camera around the room, waiting for something to appear.

"Well," I whisper to my audience, "this isn't as exciting as last night. Sorry, folks."

I keep twisting the phone around, but nothing pops up onscreen.

No creepy noises through the headphones.

No vibrations from a nearby ghost.

After ten minutes of absolutely nothing, the adrenaline and fear have worn off. I glance to the comments on my monitor. Only a few people are commenting this late, but the thoughts are unanimous: **BORING.**

And we already have two unfollows.

My gut drops.

"Okay," I say. "This game wants us to explore a bit? Fine. I guess it makes sense that it wouldn't make the ghosts come to me. I'll have to go find them. Sorta like *Pokémon Go*. So, let's see if there's anything hiding in the basement. Just give me one sec . . ."

I fiddle with the computer cameras and monitor, adjusting them away so they take in the basement. Then I get out of the seat and walk around to the other side of the desk, standing close to the center of the room.

"Can you still see me?" I wave, and watch my recorded reflection wave back. "Okay, well, I can't go that far tonight. Sorry. Still grounded. But hopefully Monday night I'll have Butterfly back, and we can do this in style."

I focus back on my phone and start slowly walking around the room, shining my flashlight around since there isn't night vision on my camera.

There's something about standing in the middle of the dark space that makes me feel more vulnerable.

My phone vibrates faintly.

My pulse begins to rise. My skin breaks out in a cold sweat.

"Okay, it's vibrating. Something is near."

I head toward the far end of the basement.

The vibration doesn't change—low and faint and barely there. I swear I cover every inch of our basement. I poke in the closets. I peer in the cupboards. I even—quickly—look under the sofa.

Nothing.

Just the low vibration that tells me there *should* be something nearby. Maybe the ghost is in another room?

Or worse, maybe the game has glitched out entirely.

After a few more moments, I sigh.

"Maybe the ghosts aren't out tonight," I say.

I wander around the basement for a few more minutes.

Nothing changes.

My fear is replaced with disappointment.

With a huge sigh, I head back over to the computer and face the camera.

"Sorry, folks. Looks like I'm not going to find anything down here. But please don't give up on us! Rather than do another solo show tomorrow, I'll be back Monday night, and this time I'll have Butterfly with me. We'll definitely find some ghosts, I promise!"

I turn off the computer and stash my headphones.

I do one more quick sweep of the basement with the flashlight and camera. But nothing is there. Even the vibration has stopped.

I turn off my phone and trudge silently upstairs.

Tonight was a dud. Next time, I'll bring in Rochelle. We need to be able to explore more. And if she's holding the portable camera, we can go anywhere we want.

I just have to hope we don't lose all our followers before then.

MONDAY
Day Four

OMG OMG OMG YOU HAVE TO CALL ME IMMEDIATELY

Rochelle's text is the first thing I see when my parents finally relinquish my phone Monday morning.

That, and about a dozen others like it, all from her.

My in-box, too, shows a few dozen new emails, but I call Rochelle before checking. Normally I'd just text, because who calls anymore? Then again, she only tells me to call when something is wrong. I hope she's okay.

My heart races as I wait for her to pick up. I'm walking out the door, the sunshine bright and a crisp cool autumn morning surrounding me. For once, I don't mind that it's Monday. I was actually excited when I woke up this morning.

Not because I'm going back to school.

Because tonight, we're going to stream.

Unless something happened to her.

"*Finally!*" Rochelle exclaims when she answers. "I thought I was going to lose my mind waiting for you to call."

"What's wrong?" I ask immediately.

"Wrong? What do you mean *wrong*?"

"I mean you only ask me to call in an emergency," I say. The last time she had me call, her brother, Jacob, had gotten into an accident on his bike and had broken his leg.

"This *is* an emergency!" she says. She pauses, my breath hitches. *"Have you checked our feed?"*

"No," I say, confused. "I called you the moment I got my phone back. Why, what's going on? Did we lose all our followers?"

"The exact opposite!" she exclaims. "Bea, we got *five hundred followers* since Saturday. Our channel is lit! How in the world did you do it?"

"What are you talking about?" I ask. My head is spinning. *Five hundred followers?* "How? The last video was of me doing absolutely nothing, and I didn't even stream yesterday."

Rochelle laughs.

"Good one, Bea. Keep up the act. I guess it's better if I don't know. But you're going to have to tell me how you did it. You can't keep secrets like that from your best friend and cohost."

"Did *what*?" I ask. My confusion is quickly turning to aggravation. It feels like she's playing a trick on me. "What are you talking about?"

"Your last stream!" she exclaims. "Ugh, just, you know what? Where are you?"

I glance around and tell her what street I'm on.

"Okay," she says. "I'll meet you there in a few minutes. Just don't go anywhere. And be prepared to reveal your tricks, O master magician."

She hangs up.

I stand there, staring at my phone, wondering what in the world she's talking about.

Then, because there's nothing better to do, I pull up my email.

Most of the messages are notifications from the stream. User comments. And donations.

"What in the world is going on?" I whisper to myself. A passing kid clearly hears me, but I ignore his raised eyebrow.

I start browsing through the comments.

SCARIEST. GAME. EVER.

YOU NEARLY HAD ME THERE.

HOW? WHAT??!!

SCREAMING.

I AM DEAD.

I feel like I'm trapped in some sort of strange waking dream.

Not only are the comments and subscribers rolling

in, but we made almost a hundred dollars in donations.

What in the world are they going on about?

I was just walking around an empty basement.

Nothing appeared.

Unless . . .

Despite the warm sun, chills crawl over me.

What if I wasn't alone down there after all?

But that would mean the game isn't just a game. That would mean . . .

"Boo!" Rochelle says, leaping on me from behind.

I scream and nearly fall to the ground, causing a few kids to look over at us. Rochelle cracks up laughing.

"Oh, come on, don't pretend to be jumpy. You're the new Mistress of Horror now, after all!"

"Rochelle," I say, breathing heavily. "What. Are. You. Talking. About?"

"The ghost!" she yells out. "The Devouring Woman!"

I'm shaking my head, and it's clear my confusion is just exasperating her. She thinks it's an act.

It's not.

"There wasn't . . . Nothing appeared when I was in the basement," I say. "That's why I didn't stream last night. I wanted to wait for you, so we could wander around and find more ghosts." Even though I wanted to stream last night—I hadn't realized a day could feel *so dang long*. And boring.

But Rochelle is just rolling her eyes.

"Yeah, yeah," she says. "Look, if you don't want to tell me in public, fine. I get it. Prying eyes and all. But I have to know how you did it. I mean, did you see how many followers we got? If we keep this up, we're going to be famous!" She pulls out her phone and opens an app. "Look! People have even uploaded a clip on social media."

She holds her phone in front of me and hits play.

It's me, walking around the basement, scanning the room with my flashlight and phone.

"I seriously can't believe you had that sort of creativity in you," Rochelle says as I stare at the recording. "I mean, what a way to hook people! I just wish you'd told me. I could have done some promo."

But I'm not listening to her ramble excitedly.

I'm watching the video.

The video of me in the empty basement.

Trying to find the source of my vibrating phone.

Trying to find the ghost that didn't exist.

Except . . .

There's a blur on the screen.

The palest mirage of pale blue.

Following behind me.

Always behind me.

And as I walk back to the camera to turn it off, disappointment clear on my face, the blur rises up from the ground.

> Towers over my shoulder.
> Becomes more than a blur.

>> Becomes a face with shadowed eye sockets

>>> and a wide,
>>> gaping
>>> mouth.

The Devouring Woman.
Impossible.
She was behind me the whole time.

12

"You don't understand," I tell Rochelle at lunch that day. "I'm not making this up. I didn't manipulate that footage."

Rochelle still doesn't believe me. But who can blame her?

Here I am, the horror fan trying to convince her best friend that a stupid indie phone game has somehow unleashed a ghost into my basement.

I'd think it was a practical joke, too.

"Right, right," she says. "If you say so. But come on, don't make me wait any longer! I want to see the app!"

All weekend, I thought I'd be relieved when I finally got my phone back. But now, it almost feels like a wild animal—I want to keep it near so I'm not caught by surprise, but I also don't want to be around it if I don't have to. It feels dangerous.

Begrudgingly, I pull the phone from my pocket and hand it over.

Once more, even though I turned it off when

classes started, the phone is on and the app is running in the background. Rochelle pulls up **DARK**[room] and immediately starts panning the camera around the crowded cafeteria.

I watch her nervously.

I can't get the image of the Devouring Woman out of my head.

Was she really in the basement the whole time, watching me? Was she following me?

And wait—what am I even thinking? This is a game. This is just a stupid game.

I bet some viewer *manipulated* the video and posted it. Deepfake. That's a thing, right?

I can't truly believe that the phone sees ghosts.

Or, worse, *summoned* them.

"Hmmm," Rochelle says after a while. "I don't see anything."

"Maybe they only come out at night?" I suggest.

"Maybe. Which, hey—we're still on to stream tonight, yeah?"

I'm about to say I'm not sure, when I realize there's someone else standing beside us.

Rochelle glances over my shoulder and rolls her eyes. That's how I know who it is before I even look.

"I see you started a new game," he says.

Rochelle's brother, Jacob.

My heart leaps into my throat before I even turn around. Jacob's in the same grade as us, with dark skin and curly black hair. He had a growth spurt a few summers ago, and went from being the awkward dorky boy who followed Rochelle and me around to being the tall and muscly nerd who somehow managed to learn how to play soccer in between his dungeon-crawling MMOs.

He also still tried to follow us around, until Rochelle got annoyed with him and told him to buzz off. Which is probably for the best, because ever since little Jacob grew up, I've had a hard time being around him. I'm not usually tongue-tied, but around him, I am.

"Stalking us, much?" Rochelle asks.

Jacob shrugs. "You know I'm subscribed to your stream. Gotta support my little sis."

Rochelle glowers at him.

"Besides," he continues, "one of my buddies texted me about it last night. Said you'd found some cool new indie game that no one else could play. So I had to tune in. I have to admit, it was pretty creepy."

"I, um," I stammer. Thankfully, Jacob catches sight of the phone screen then and saves me from making more of a fool of myself.

"Whoa, is that it?" he asks.

"Yup!" Rochelle says. She turns the screen to him.

In the camera, her visage is grayscale and eerie. She almost looks like a ghost herself. "The game everyone is talking about. We'd tell you how to get the link, but then we'd have to kill you."

Jacob laughs, and my heart beats a little faster.

"So cool," he says. "You're streaming again tonight, yeah?"

"We are indeed," Rochelle replies. "The team is back together, and we're here to hunt down some ghosts."

Jacob's smile nearly makes me faint. "Awesome. I can't wait to watch. Me and some buddies have subscribed. We're taking bets to see how long it takes you to finish off the boss." He chuckles and flushes a little bit. "I told them you'd beat it by Wednesday. But, you know, no pressure."

Then, before I can make any more of a fool of myself, he does this nervous little nod-wave thing and walks off. I watch him go.

When he's a few tables away, Rochelle cackles.

"I have never seen someone so starstruck, Beatrice," she says. "Looks like someone's got a crush!"

"What, I don't—"

"Not you, idiot. Jacob."

If my cheeks weren't flushed before, they certainly are now.

"I guess that settles it, then," she says. "I'll meet you at your place after dinner tonight. Convince your parents to let me come over. We have an audience now. As much as it weirds me out that you're in love with my brother, I suppose we can't let him down."

I nudge her slightly. She hands me back the phone.

Whatever fear I had before is vanished, overtaken by the glow from Jacob's attention.

Of course we're going to keep streaming.

We have to give our followers what they want.

13

It's surprisingly easy to convince my parents to let Rochelle come over on a school night. Thankfully, we *are* working on a history project together, so I can use that as an excuse. But after I've texted to give Rochelle the thumbs-up and I've sat down to dinner, my parents ask the question I know is coming.

"So," my dad says, "are you girls going to stream tonight?"

There's no point lying—it's not like we can hide what we're doing if we're hunting ghosts all over the house. But I've thought this through.

"I actually wanted to talk to you about that," I say.

"Oh?" Mom asks.

I nod and sit up a little straighter, setting my fork down.

"Yes," I say. "I wanted to let you know that Rochelle and I are officially paid streamers now."

"Really?" Dad asks.

"Yes. When I checked my phone this morning, I learned that the new game we started playing is quite a hit. Over the last week, we've gotten over five hundred new followers. And we've received almost a hundred dollars in donations. I was thinking we could donate some of that to the local animal shelter, if you'd help us set that up."

Technically speaking, half of that money is going to Rochelle. But they don't need to know that.

I just need them to hear the words *responsible* and *business*.

"That's . . . that's incredible, honey," Mom says.

"What game are you playing?" Dad asks. As if he'll have any clue what I'm talking about.

"It's called **DARK[room]**," I reply. "It's actually a phone app. You take pictures of ghosts in real time, so it's this really cool augmented reality sort of thing. And it's an indie game, so there's not a bunch of people playing it."

"Sounds scary," Mom says.

I nod. But rather than worrying about the Devouring Woman, all I can think of is the way Jacob smiled at me, and his promise that he'd be watching us play later.

I never really cared about attention from boys. I just wanted attention in general. But now that I have it, I realize it's pretty darn nice. I wonder if he's one of the viewers who sent a donation.

"Maybe we'll watch you stream sometime," Dad suggests.

I'm ready for this, too.

"Maybe," I tell him. "But it's pretty boring to start off. Most people are just watching to see what happens next."

After Rochelle and I have done our next stream, I'm totally planning on deleting the ones from this weekend. Or at least making them private. Just in case my parents look through our history—I don't want to get in trouble again. Not when I'm on a roll.

"Well, we won't disturb you two, then," Mom says. "Just remember to get your homework done beforehand."

"And be careful," Dad warns. "There are a lot of creeps out there."

"I know, Dad," I say.

14

There's a small, rational part of me that knows I should leave the game alone.

I should delete the app and tell Rochelle we're streaming something else. Maybe something funny. Do they even make funny games?

I mean, I know from watching horror movies that I am doing *precisely* what I've screamed at the protagonist not to do.

I'm going up into the attic to investigate the strange noise.

I'm going deeper into the woods even though I've lost the map.

I'm splitting up with the group to cover more ground.

I'm doing the obvious, stupid thing. I'm going in deeper. I'm heading toward the danger, and not away from it. I'm chasing the ghosts, rather than running away from them.

And that small, rational Beatrice is screaming out

and pounding her fists and saying, *No, you idiot! You're going to get yourself killed*.

Watching all those movies, I always told myself that if I were in that situation, I'd be smart.

I'd go to the authorities.

I'd leave the obviously haunted mansion.

I wouldn't pick up the cursed artifact.

And yet.

And yet every time I convince myself to pick up the phone and delete the app and call Rochelle and shut this down, I have another notification. Another new message. Or comment. Or donation.

The stream is popular.

And that popularity is growing.

Worse still is that every time I consider getting rid of the app, I see Jacob's smile. I hear the enthusiasm in his voice. I get the flutter of butterflies in my stomach as I imagine him tuning in, and maybe starting to fall for me. I'm already fighting down visions of him asking me to Homecoming, or having game nights cuddled up on the couch and eating pizza together. I can't help it: I have an overactive imagination.

By the time Rochelle shows up at six thirty, our stream has passed a thousand followers, and we've made almost two hundred dollars in donations. Every comment is cheering us on, demanding to know when the next episode is. Demanding to know how we did it.

Demanding to know if we're still alive, or if the Devouring Woman got us.

So.

I *am* going up into the attic.

I *am* going deeper into the woods without a map.

I *am* touching the cursed artifact.

If I don't, I fade back into obscurity before I really know recognition.

I lose Jacob before I even had him.

I have to ride this out. I have to catch this shooting star.

I have to become famous.

When Rochelle shows up, I know—as ashamed as I am to admit it—that fame is something I'd happily die for.

15

"Popcorn?" Rochelle asks.

"Check," I reply.

"Mics?"

I test the levels. "Check."

"Steadicam?"

It's not actually a Steadicam, but we've managed to rig a handheld camera to stream our feed, so Rochelle can follow me around the house as we hunt down ghosts.

"Check," I say.

"Energy drinks?"

I glance to the mini-fridge, which is freshly stocked with energy drinks and one bottle of water because my mom told me to hydrate. "Double check."

Rochelle's excitement makes me excited, just as her clear lack of fear puts me at ease.

This is just a game to her.

And that's because this *is* just a game. Just an ordinary game.

One that is going to make us very famous.

"Okay, then," she says. "You ready?"

I pull out my phone. Fully charged and connected to a spare battery, just in case. I nod.

"Let's hunt some ghosts," she tells me.

She flips the camera around to face her and stands next to me. Our faces beam back in the display. With her free hand, she leans over and hovers a finger over the computer mouse, ready to start.

"Streaming in three, two . . ."

She presses the button and instantly goes into show mode.

"Hello, ghosts and ghouls," she says. "The Ghastly Girls are back together once more for the next chilling installment of the game everyone is talking about: DARK[room]. I'm Butterfly, and I'm here with my cohost, Crimson." I give a winning smile and wave. "Since she's already on the hunt for her first ghost, we're going to let her take the wheel tonight, and I'll be your rock-steady cameraman. Well, camera*woman*.

"As you've no doubt seen on our last upload, this game is more than just a game. This game doesn't just let you take pictures of ghosts, it *unleashes them*." She shudders theatrically. "Last stream, Crimson barely made it out of her basement alive as the hunter became the hunted, and the ghostly Devouring Woman came after her. The ghost even made a surprise appearance on our feed."

She looks to me and winks. She *still* thinks it was a trick of mine.

"Tonight, we'll see if lightning can strike twice. We know the Devouring Woman is out there, but we're going to see what other ghosts we can hunt down. Wish us luck. We're going to need it."

With one final smile, she flips the camera back into normal mode and centers it on me and my phone.

"Right," I say. "I've just pulled up the game. Let's see if there's anything lurking in the dark."

I slowly scan the room with my phone, the flashlight illuminating the corners and walls. Onscreen, the basement is grainy and dark, the halo of light blindingly white. Rochelle stands behind me, keeping me and the screen in frame.

"Nothing so far. Let's walk around a bit."

My heart starts to beat fast, and I can't figure out if it's fear that nothing will happen, or fear that something *will*. Rochelle thinks the apparition on the feed was a trick—I know it wasn't—so what if it shows up now? Here? What if I look up over my phone to see the Devouring Woman staring at me?

The phone begins to vibrate, a slow pulse.

"It's vibrating," I whisper. "Something's near."

"Eep!" Rochelle says behind me. "I swear I felt something brush past my leg."

My heart flips. I dart the phone around, trying not to move too fast so Rochelle can keep everything in frame.

Onscreen, I see something scramble out from the corner.

A dark shadow like a bat or a scuttling spider.

It darts

up

the wall

and freezes

in the upper corner.

"What is it?" Rochelle asks.

"I don't know," I reply. It isn't the Devouring Woman. That much I know.

This shape quivers in place, a shadowy blob. It doesn't move, just waits there, shuddering.

I center the screen on it, and the phone vibrates stronger. No name appears.

I take a picture.

Light flashes, but nothing else happens. The blob stays in the corner onscreen. I glance past my phone and am grateful to see that there isn't anything *actually* there. It's all in the game.

"I think we need to move closer," Rochelle suggests.

"Right," I say.

I take a step forward.

The shadow shudders.

Another step.

My skin breaks out in goose bumps as the phone vibrates stronger, pulsing a warning, telling me to turn around, to run, as the shadow stretches out slowly.

Another step.

"Beatrice, look!" Rochelle gasps.

She doesn't have to tell me. I can't take my eyes off it.

The rippling shadow writhes onscreen, and now other shapes appear within it. White dots in the black. Gnashing. Sharp. Jagged.

Teeth.

Dozens and dozens of teeth.

Some sharp, some blunt, some cracked and rotted and others pristine, some formed like mouths and others like talons.

Finally, a name appears onscreen

THE TOOTH FAIRY

"That doesn't look like a fairy to me," Rochelle whispers.

The moment she speaks, the shadow unfolds a series of spindly, spiderlike legs. And two wicked-looking pincers made of cat's teeth.

It snaps its pincers forward, extending them at my face, and I take a step back on impulse.

Instantly I crash into Rochelle, who curses and stumbles, nearly falling to the ground.

"Watch it!" she yelps.

But I'm already focusing the phone on the ghost, which darts across the ceiling so fast I can't track it.

"Where did it go?" I ask. I scan the room, but there isn't anything there. The phone still vibrates, but it's so faint I can barely feel it over the pulse of my own blood.

"It went toward the stairs," Rochelle says. "At least, I think it did."

"Come on," I say. My parents are probably reading in bed already—their nightly ritual—so the downstairs should be free.

We head toward the basement steps and make our way up into the living room.

Behind me, I swear I hear the Devouring Woman moan.

16

The living room feels quiet. Too quiet.

And, okay, it's *my* living room. I've been down here in the dark, like, a million times, and I *know* my parents are awake upstairs reading. It's only eight. But it still feels like stepping into a haunted house. The lights are off and the streetlights beyond make the room look grayscale even in real life.

It's also not my imagination—it is *freezing* here.

Rochelle trails behind me, keeping me in focus while I scan the living room with the camera.

The sheer white curtains hang limp like waiting ghosts.

The shadows beneath the sofa scuttle and shift as my light plays over them.

But there is no sign of the Tooth Fairy.

"Where did it go?" Rochelle whispers.

"I don't know," I reply.

Something shifts to my right, and I jerk my phone

over just in time to catch *something* scuttle from the ceiling to beneath the sofa.

"I think we got our answer," Rochelle says.

I swallow. I really don't want to look under the sofa, but the phone is pulsing and we're still filming. So I drop to my knees and angle myself down to look into the dusty shadows beneath.

At first, I only see darkness. A heavy, physical darkness that eats up the light.

The phone vibrates stronger.

As does a low groaning that fills the room. Now that I'm not wearing headphones, I'm not entirely convinced it's coming from the phone.

The darkness shifts.

And a face
appears
in the shadows.
Her face.
Her shadowed eye sockets.
Her broken, gaping mouth.

DEVOURING WOMAN

"OMG," Rochelle gasps behind me. "It's her!"

The Devouring Woman's attention snaps from me to Rochelle. Before I can warn my friend, the ghost lurches forward.

I lunge to the side as the Devouring Woman attacks. But she isn't after me.

She's after Rochelle.

The Devouring Woman's groans are so loud I fully expect my parents to come down. She roars in anger as she scuttles toward Rochelle. And without my camera, Rochelle can't see a thing. She just crouches there, still filming me, though there's a vacant look in her eyes. She seems entranced.

"Look out!" I whisper-yell.

The Devouring Woman rears up beside Rochelle, towering over her. The ghost's mouth widens, the darkness within unfurling into a long gray tongue that curls around Rochelle's neck like a rope. I know in that moment that the Devouring Woman will eat her if I don't act fast. Why isn't Rochelle moving? What's going on?

Some instinct within me takes over.

I bring up the camera and take a picture.

Light flashes.

The phone vibrates wildly.

The Devouring Woman shrieks and the camera pulses.

Onscreen, three words appear that make a wave of relief roll through me.

DEVOURING WOMAN CAPTURED

But the relief is short-lived.

I lower my phone and rush over to Rochelle, who crouches there in shock.

"Are you okay?" I ask.

Rochelle doesn't respond right away. She's staring at the shadows with a dull expression in her eyes, like she's a million miles away. I put a hand on her shoulder and she jolts. When her eyes focus on me, it looks like she's seeing me for the first time.

"What . . . what happened?" she asks.

"I . . . the Devouring Woman. She attacked you."

She nearly ate you! Why didn't you move when I told you to?

Rochelle shakes her head. Then a new urgency lights up her face.

"Did we get it on camera?"

"I don't know," I say. She's still holding the hand-held, but since we were facing the wrong way, I doubt she caught anything from my phone screen. "What happened to you? It's like you were a zombie for a moment there."

She holds the camera out a bit so it can take in the two of us.

"I don't know," she says. Her voice wavers. "I was watching through the camera. I saw the ghost on your screen. But then . . ."

She trails off, and her eyes get that vacant look again.

"And then what?" I press.

"And then I heard a voice," she says softly. "Telling me everything was going to be okay. It was a woman's voice. And the room just sort of faded away, along with the fear."

A shudder rips through me. Did the Devouring Woman entrance my friend? How would that even be possible?

"She nearly ate you," I whisper.

"Good thing you were there, then," Rochelle replies. As if nearly getting eaten by a ghost from a game is an everyday thing. "Did you capture her?"

"Yeah. Do you . . . do you want to keep playing?"

Without missing a beat, she says, "Yeah. I think we have to. I mean, I don't know if we have a choice." She takes a deep, shaky breath. "I didn't want to believe it, but I think you were right. I think this game *does* release ghosts. I think this is real."

17

My heart stops beating for a moment when she says it.

"You believe me?" I ask.

She nods. She's still capturing all this on camera.

"I didn't want to at first," she admits. "I thought you had been making it up, you know? Somehow put the ghost in after you filmed. But whatever that was . . ." She shivers again. "That wasn't a game. I *felt* her standing beside me. Felt her words inside my brain. You're sure that wasn't coming from the game?"

I shake my head. "All I heard was her horrible groaning."

"Then she was real. *This* is real." She looks to the camera, then to me. "The game really did release ghosts, and we have to capture them before they hurt someone."

I don't want to agree with her. My rational brain is still trying to click things together in the way they *should* go. But it doesn't line up.

How could a game put Rochelle into a trance?

How could a game make a ghost appear on a video stream?

I think back to the discussion boards I read. Warning people off. Maybe they weren't a marketing ploy after all. Maybe the warnings had been posted by real gamers. Real kids.

Maybe they really were dead, beaten by the game.

I try to push all that out of my mind. *This is a video game.* Video games don't kill you. That sort of thing just doesn't happen in real life.

But now that Rochelle believes it's true, it's harder for me to convince myself it's all just in my head.

"Right," Rochelle says. She stands up straighter and takes on an authoritative tone. "There are six ghosts left. And the final ghost appears Thursday, right?"

"I think that's what it meant. But maybe the final ghost will appear sooner?"

"Hard to say. What's important is that we start picking off the other ghosts. So, Crimson, let's hunt some spirits. That creepy Tooth Fairy thing has to be somewhere."

I nod and bring up my phone. I don't really want to do this anymore. I want to put my phone away and never play DARK[room] again.

But if the ghosts are out there, then it means the

game's warning might also be true: They don't go away when I turn off the phone.

I either win, or we all lose.

I take a deep breath. Try to visualize the hundreds of people watching. To them, it's just a show.

To us, it's starting to feel all too real.

I scan the room with my phone again. Nothing.

Not even the slightest vibration.

"Looks like we have to explore," I say.

"Maybe we should head outside?" Rochelle recommends.

For some reason, the suggestion fills me with dread. Not because I'm scared of going outside at night. But because I'm scared that going outside might, I don't know, release the ghosts into the world. I don't want them stuck in my house with me, but I also don't want to endanger anyone else. Especially when the only defense is an app no one has heard of.

Rochelle clearly notices my hesitation, but she must take it as a sign of fear. "Actually, let's try the kitchen," she says. Then she grins. "I could use a snack."

We make our way into the kitchen, me in the lead once more. I scan the room frantically, but there's still no sign of anything.

"I wonder if it's timed," Rochelle says. "You know, so not all the ghosts show up at once."

"Didn't you say you thought this was real?" I ask.

Rochelle catches herself. "I do. I mean, I think so. But that doesn't mean it won't follow, like, game logistics."

"Maybe," I say, glancing over my shoulder at her. "I sort of hope not, though."

"Why?"

"Because in games, the first enemies you fight are the weakest, and they scale up as you get more experience and weapons. But this is real life. We aren't getting any more experience, and the only weapon is this."

I shake my phone.

"Did you get points or anything?" she asks. "Maybe you can upgrade its features."

I examine the display. "No," I say. "But, wait, actually . . ."

There's a small 1 in the corner now. I'd missed it before—it blends into the background. When I click it, an image of a list appears, numbered one through seven.

1. ~~DEVOURING WOMAN~~
2. XXX
3. TOOTH FAIRY
4. XXX

5. XXX
6. XXX
7. XXX

"Huh," Rochelle says, peering over my shoulder. "I guess that's . . . sort of handy."

When I click the line with the Devouring Woman, a new screen pops up. It shows her picture, along with a short bio.

**THE DEVOURING WOMAN'S ENDLESS HUNGER MEANS SHE IS THE FIRST TO SEEK OUT NEW FLESH. ONCE SHE HAS YOUR SCENT, SHE WILL NEVER STOP THE HUNT.
X-CAPTURED-X**

"Does it say anything about the Tooth Fairy?" Rochelle asks, leaning over my shoulder.

Something lands on my screen. Crumbs. I glance over at her to see she's eating cookies. Isn't she taking this seriously?

I go back to the list and click on the Tooth Fairy. The shadowy, tooth-filled mass appears next to its bio.

**MISSING A TOOTH? BEWARE THIS GHOST.
NOT MISSING A TOOTH? YOU WILL BE.**

ITS SWEET TOOTH IS PAIN.
AND YOURS TASTES DELICIOUS.

"That's it?" Rochelle asks. Still juggling the phone that's recording all this, she leans over and clicks on the other numbers, but nothing else comes up. "Not exactly helpful, is it?"

"No," I say. "And no sign of weapons upgrades either. So we better hope the ghosts don't get harder."

"Definitely," she agrees. "Though it looks like you've skipped a ghost. The Tooth Fairy is number three."

I'm reminded of the first night I opened the app. I remember seeing the Devouring Woman, but there had been something else. A shadow along the ceiling.

The thought that there might have been more than one monster in the room with me sends a fresh wave of chills over my skin.

"Only one way to find out," I say. "Come on."

I don't make it two steps, however, when a noise stops me in my tracks.

Giggling.

Coming from behind me.

My phone starts vibrating harder.

"Rochelle," I whisper. "Was that laughter coming from the phone?"

"I . . . I don't know," she says.

I turn around to face her.

She appears in the camera screen.

Along with two

other

figures.

Small boys with shock-white hair stand on each side of her. They barely reach her hips, and their heads are tilted down.

"Don't move," I say. "There are two ghosts right by you."

Rochelle gasps theatrically and goes stock-still.

I aim my camera down toward one of the boys.

Text appears below his face.

THE TWINS

Before I can take his picture, he and his brother look up at me.

Their eyes are black holes.

My phone vibrates so hard it nearly falls out of my hand.

I take a picture. Light flashes.

And all chaos breaks loose.

18

I'm nearly blinded by the bright flash of light.

"Ow!" Rochelle yells out.

Something smacks into me and knocks me to the floor. My phone skids out of my hand; without its light, the room is nearly pitch-black. Stars swim in my vision as I struggle to stand up, struggle to find my phone.

Any second I expect to feel the tiny hands of the Twins grabbing at me.

Any second I expect to see their ghastly eyeless faces rear up in front of me.

"Rochelle, are you okay? Do you see them?"

She's fumbling around beside me, mumbling angrily as she searches for the camera that she dropped.

But then something even scarier than ghosts appears in the kitchen.

The light flicks on, and my dad is standing in the entryway.

"What in the world is going on in here?" he asks.

Rochelle is getting to her feet, the camera a few

inches from her hand. I am still crouched on the floor.

My phone is nowhere in sight. We are defenseless. Worse, my dad is clearly upset.

"I—we—" I stammer.

"Just getting into our game, Mr. Robinson!"

My dad looks at his watch, and then at us.

"It's nearly nine thirty," he says. "I think it's time for you to go home, Rochelle."

"But we just started streaming!" I blurt out.

His glare tells me not to push my luck. I might be getting donations now, but I'm still fresh out of being grounded.

"Sorry, Dad," I say. "We were just at a scary part. I didn't mean to be rude."

He nods.

"I appreciate that. But you girls have school in the morning. You can stream tomorrow."

It's definitely not a good idea to push him now. I have to stay in his good graces. *We* have to stay in his good graces.

If he takes my phone away again, who knows what will happen?

Which . . .

I look around. No sign of my phone anywhere. Did it slide behind the fridge?

Or worse: Did one of the Twins take it?

"Do you see my phone?" I ask.

Dad shakes his head. "I'm sure it will show up in the morning. Come on, girls. Call it a night."

I sigh, but there's clearly no budging him. Rochelle has recovered her own camera and now turns it around to face her.

Great, I think. *The whole internet got to hear me be called out by my dad.* If I wasn't so worried about the ghosts, I'd want to sink through the floor in embarrassment.

"Right, you heard the man," Rochelle says. "Butterfly and Crimson are signing off for the night. One ghost down, six more to go. Let us know in the comments which one you thought was the scariest, as well as any guesses as to what the remaining mystery ghosts might be."

She doesn't even give me a chance to sign off, just ends the recording and smiles charmingly at my dad.

"Thanks again for letting me come over, Mr. Robinson," she says. "I hope we didn't disturb you too much."

"It's okay, Rochelle," Dad replies. Rochelle is my dad's favorite—he could never stay mad at her. "Just keep it quiet next time."

Which means he's okay with there being a next time!

Dad heads upstairs and Rochelle I head down to the basement to grab her stuff. We keep the lights on the entire time.

"Are you going to be okay tonight?" I ask her.

She looks at me strangely. "Of course I will. Why wouldn't I be?"

"Because of what we saw. What you experienced. The Devouring Woman . . ."

"Oh, that," she says flippantly, slinging her backpack over her shoulder. "That was acting, thank you."

"Wait, what?"

"Yeah," she says. She starts walking toward the stairs as if she didn't just drop a bomb. "We had to put on a good show. I mean, what else was I supposed to do? You were freaking out and it would have looked strange if I was just standing there all calm."

"But you said you felt her," I say. "You said you heard her voice."

"Great improv, right? I swear, if streaming doesn't work out for me, maybe I should become an actor."

She's halfway up the basement steps. I haven't moved a muscle. I'm still standing beside all the recording equipment.

She lied.

And maybe she didn't think she was lying to me, but she was. Because I was telling the truth about seeing and feeling and hearing the ghosts. I thought she had experienced it all, too.

"Are you gonna stay down here all night?" she asks.

"No, I'm coming."

I hurry and follow her up the steps.

I stay by her side until she's out the front door, but for the first time since her arrival, I feel horribly alone.

19

That night, I dream I'm being followed.

The halls of my house stretch before and
behind me.

Shadows before me.

Shadows behind me.

I can't tell where I'm going.

I can't tell if it ends.

I can't stop running.

If I do, she will find me.

If I do, she will kill me.

I run harder.

My breath burns.

My feet ache.

I didn't know dreams could hurt.

This one does.

I turn a corner. Reach a hall lined with windows.

And there she is.

Floating in a pool of moonlight.

Facing away.

At first, I think it is the Devouring Woman.

Her long black hair reaches her ankles.

   Her ankles, which float inches from the
      floor.

Her dress is white, pure as pearls.

   White, and knotted with thick lengths
      of rope.

She turns.

   So

   slowly

   she

   turns.

And when she faces me, I realize she is
   beautiful.

   Her skin flawless.

   Her red lips perfect.

   Her dark eyes kind.

At first.

Then she floats forward.

The moment she slips from the shaft of
   moonlight
   she
   begins
   to change.

      Her face shrivels and becomes
         corpse-like.

Her hands elongate into bony claws.

I take a terrified step backward.

She raises her skeletal hand.

Opens her mouth.

And screams.

×✗×

I jolt awake.

Fumble with my covers that are wrapped tight around me, constricting me. When I realize it was just a dream—just a stupid stress dream—I let out a sigh and flop back on the bed.

I need to stop eating so much sugar before going to sleep.

And maybe stop playing horror games.

"Oh, this is no game, Beatrice," comes a voice.

I turn to the closet.

The door creaks open.

A skeletal hand curls around the frame.

It's her. The ghost from my dream. It's *her*.

"No," I gasp. "This isn't real. This isn't real."

"I'm coming for you, Beatrice." The door opens a little wider. I can see her silhouette against my clothes. Can smell the rotting of her flesh.

"No," I say. "No, I don't want to play anymore. I'm done with this game. I'm done!"

She cackles. The door opens wider.

"You don't get to stop playing," she taunts. *"Not until we have finished playing with you!"*

The closet door bursts open.

I scream out.

Flinch back.

Hide my eyes.

But nothing happens.

Moments pass.

Finally, I lower my arm. Peer out.

The closet door is closed.

The ghost is nowhere to be seen.

My heart hammers so loudly in my chest I think it's going to explode.

Was that a dream? I wonder wildly. *A dream within a dream?*

I wait there for ages. I don't move. Don't speak. Don't call out to my parents, even though I really want to.

I still don't know if that was a dream, or reality.

Finally, when my breathing slows, I convince myself it was just a nightmare. A very, very realistic nightmare.

Maybe I should give up the game after all.

Maybe fame isn't worth scaring myself this much.

We'll talk about it at school. I'm sure I can convince Rochelle to pick up something else.

Feeling slightly better, I lie back down and settle my arm beneath my pillow.

Wait.

There's something there.

I reach under . . .

and pull out my phone.

TUESDAY
Day Five

20

I don't fall back asleep.

I debate what I should do until the sun comes up.

There is no way the phone could have just ended up under my pillow, no way one of my parents came in while I was sleeping and snuck it under there—not that they would.

The only way it could have gotten there is if a ghost had brought it to me, which is probably one of the most ridiculous things I've ever thought, but I can't stop suspecting it's true.

What was it the ghost had said in my dreams? *You don't get to stop playing . . .*

I almost delete the app. But then I check my email, and I see the hundreds—literally *hundreds*—of notifications in my inbox.

We have two *thousand* new followers.

And we have made nearly five hundred dollars in new donations.

Our feed is littered with comments, most of them

responding to Rochelle's question about what ghost they thought was scariest, and what they think is coming next. I'm amazed at how many people have chimed in, how many people are watching.

There's also a string of texts. From a number I don't know.

> Hey Bea. Hope you don't mind. I got your number from Rochelle. You were great tonight. Hope you didn't get in trouble. Looking forward to another stream. See you in class.

> Also sorry. This is so awkward.

> It's Jacob, btw.

> Okay, bye.

My cheeks flush.

Jacob.

I can't even be mad that Rochelle gave him my number without asking. I mean, she knows I would have been too embarrassed to say yes anyway. It's adorable how awkward Jacob is over text.

I sit there for a few moments, rereading his texts, and it's like all the fear just washes away for an instant.

This is the first time a boy has texted me. Well, the first time a boy I *like* has texted me, and it's pretty clear he likes me, too, otherwise why would he have gone to the effort of getting my number from Rochelle?

I text him back.

It's a stupid first text but it's all I can think of this early. I close my messaging app.

And there, on my home screen, is **DARK[room]**.

I hesitate.

My finger hovers over it.

I should delete the game. If I was smart, I would delete the game. There's a very good chance that it has released very real ghosts, and that I'm in very real danger.

But then my phone buzzes again.

Another email.

Another notification from our stream.

Another donation.

I sigh and start to get ready for school.

I'll keep the app. For now.

It's not like anyone has gotten hurt.

21

I feel like a celebrity as I walk down the halls.

Kids I don't even know stop to talk to me. Upperclassmen that only a few days ago would have ignored me or insulted me now stop to get my selfie, and not to post as some mean meme.

They ask me how I got the app, since apparently the game's creators have gone dark since I started streaming (I guess there goes my hope of getting some sort of sponsorship from them). They ask when I'm going to stream again. They ask me to pull up the app to show them what it looks like in real life.

One of them even asks me to sign the back of their phone, which I think is ridiculous, but, hey, whatever, it's their phone.

I'm stopped so many times I barely make it to my first class.

I flop down in the desk next to Rochelle. Despite the fact that I'm still hurt she doesn't believe the game is real, she's still my best friend.

"It's wild out there, isn't it?" she asks.

"Dude, someone asked me to sign their phone," I reply.

She smiles wide. "This was the best idea we've ever had. We're *famous*. And this is only the beginning! We *have* to stream tonight. Which, oh, did you find your phone?"

"Yeah. You'll never believe—"

But our teacher calls us to attention, and my words are cut short.

You'll never believe how I found it. It's almost like the ghosts want *me to play.*

I can barely focus during class.

Not only because I keep catching sight of Jacob from the corner of my eye, but because every few seconds my phone buzzes in my pocket. And I *know* I put it on DO NOT DISTURB. I just have to hope our teacher doesn't hear. We're supposed to leave phones in our lockers, but after mine showed up on my pillow this morning, I don't trust letting it out of my sight.

I wonder what the notifications are. Maybe they're more followers.

More donations.

More fame.

"Miss Robinson," our teacher Mr. Hinckley says

to me, "would you *kindly* turn off your phone or risk having it confiscated?"

My cheeks flush in embarrassment.

"Sorry, Mr. Hinckley," I say. "I thought I had."

A few kids chuckle as I pull out my phone and switch it off.

Before the screen goes black, I realize that it hasn't been buzzing from emails or notifications from my stream.

A pop-up banner has appeared onscreen. From DARK[room].

A GHOST IS NEAR. YOU ARE IN DANGER.

My heart skips a beat as the phone goes black, buzzing one final time.

I tell myself it was just a ploy to get me to play. The ghosts wouldn't follow me here. And they wouldn't do anything in the light of day.

"Much better," Mr. Hinckley says. "Now, as I was saying . . ."

He goes back to teaching as though nothing out of the ordinary has happened, but I can't focus.

Rochelle gives me a look that clearly asks, *What's up?*

I just shrug.

She doesn't believe the game is real, and she isn't going to believe it if I say something now.

A part of me almost wishes a ghost *was* near. A ghost she could see in real life. Then maybe she'd start to believe me.

We're sitting at lunch when my phone begins to ring. At full volume.

It's just Rochelle and me at the end of our usual spot, though I keep noticing Jacob looking our way, and a few kids have stopped by the table to congratulate us on our stream. But now, people are stopping and staring. Including my least favorite bullies, Claire and Kaitlin.

"I thought you turned your phone off in class," Rochelle says.

"I did," I reply, my gut sinking.

I reach in and pull it out.

"Did you turn it on again?" Rochelle asks.

"No," I say.

It's DARK[room].

A notification screen has popped up and it continues to ring at full volume.

THE GHOSTS ARE NEAR.
PLAY NOW OR PAY THE PRICE.

I try to silence the phone, but the volume control doesn't do anything and the power button isn't turning it off.

"Make it stop!" hisses Rochelle.

Although we're technically allowed to have our phones at lunch, they're supposed to be on silent.

"I'm trying!" I reply. "It's glitching out."

"Maybe you have to play to make it stop," says someone's voice.

I look over my shoulder. Jacob.

He's standing behind me, along with a few other kids. Oddly enough, they all look excited.

I look to Rochelle.

She shrugs and pulls out her own phone.

"Okay," she says, pointing her phone at me. "I'm recording." Louder, she says, "Sorry we weren't able to livestream this, ghosts and ghouls. Crimson's phone started acting up in school, and we have no choice but to play! Hopefully it's scary enough to merit an upload." She stands up and sidles behind me, so she can capture the phone screen.

I give one last look around the gathering crowd, and hit **PLAY**.

Someone *whoop*s behind me, making me jump, but they're just excited to be watching this live, which feels strange in and of itself. I mean, I guess I've been playing for an audience the last few nights, but a *live* audience watching right behind my shoulder? Including the way-too-cute Jacob? Very strange. It feels like being onstage, and even though I want to be popular, that's always warred with my natural stage fright.

But my focus immediately shifts when the game screen comes on.

Instantly the screen crackles with film grain, and the lunchroom becomes black-and-white. I slowly cast the camera around, taking in the kids ignoring us, the kids watching us, and a few teachers who can't seem to decide if they should be doing something about this or not.

I just have to hope I can catch this ghost before the teachers catch on.

It's very different playing in a crowded room. It's much, much more difficult. Every time someone moves, I think it's a ghost. I can't hear anything over the noise and laughter of my classmates, so I can't tell if there are any ghosts calling out. The only thing I have to go by is the vibration on my phone.

Which, since I've started the game, has been buzzing softly.

"There's something here," I say, scanning again. "I can feel it."

Someone cries out excitedly behind us, causing a jump from me and an angry glare from Rochelle and a muted *sorry* from whoever it was.

Okay, I already really don't like playing for a live crowd.

Something shifts at the corner of my vision and I flip the camera around, face it toward a group of kids seated nearby. A pale blue ghost darts from under their table so fast I barely catch it. The moment I try to follow it, another flash runs off under the tables. Two ghosts.

Oh no.

"Oooh," comes Jacob's voice. "I think it's the Twins!"

And he's right, I know he's right.

Because now I hear giggling coming from the phone, and every once in a while the ghostly duo will pause and I'll catch sight of their tiny figures. The shock-white hair, the empty eyes. The moment I spot them and center them in the camera, they dart off again, hiding under tables and behind my classmates' legs. But they're always out of reach, a step from being out of sight.

"Why aren't they getting closer?" Rochelle asks.

"Maybe we have to follow," I reply.

I awkwardly stand while still panning the phone around, and Rochelle hurries to follow me. We have to catch these ghosts soon—a few of the teachers are look-ing at me suspiciously, and I know they're going to confiscate my phone if I make too much of a scene. I catch sight of one Twin. The boy actually *waves* at me as he pauses, his shadowed eyes seeming to pierce into my soul as he smiles. He giggles and runs off. I follow.

He darts between classmates, and I try to navigate the crowded cafeteria, which is hard since I have to keep my eyes on my phone.

The ghost boy ducks under a table. I can just make out his smiling face between the chairs.

"Got you," I whisper.

I center the phone. Ready the shot. The phone vibrates strongly, a clear sign I've got him in frame.

And right before I take a picture, someone shoves into me, making me fumble and nearly drop the phone.

"Did you *ask* permission to take her picture, creep?" the girl asks. I look over. Kaitlin.

She glares at me, hands on her hips. Rochelle and the others stand around us, watching the confrontation with uneasy stares.

I look back to the phone. The boy is still there, but now his brother has joined him. They stand on either side of the girl I'd been about to take a picture of. Claire.

They both point to her in a perfectly mirrored movement.

Then they raise their other hands to their necks and make a slicing motion.

I gasp.

And the ghosts disappear.

22

"I seriously thought she was about to burst a blood vessel," Rochelle says. "I've never seen Kaitlin so mad."

"I know," I say. "I don't know what was scarier—waiting for her or Claire to punch me, or the ghost Twins."

We're maybe a block away from school, walking to my house. I haven't actually asked my parents if Rochelle could come over. I figure it's easier to beg forgiveness than ask permission, especially after the mess we made in the kitchen last night. Also, I know it will be harder for them to turn Rochelle away. Those dimples, man. They work wonders.

"Right?" she asks. "Thankfully we got everything on film. We can upload it as a special feature for our paid subscribers tonight. I wonder if we'll see the Twins again. Creepy kids just freak me out, you know?"

I nod, but that's not what has me so worried. Rochelle apparently didn't see the Twins gesturing threateningly at Claire. And what could I say? That

I'm worried the game is going to somehow hurt a school bully? She already thinks I'm just pulling one over on her, that I'm just *performing* by saying it's all real.

The ghosts had disappeared after the confrontation in the lunchroom, and my phone had been silent for the rest of the day, for which I was thankful. I didn't need to get in trouble again—if my parents got another call from my school about me being on my phone, I could kiss my streaming days goodbye, no matter how many donations we'd gotten and how much I'd channeled into the humane society. The only thing that *didn't* disappear was the mean looks from Claire and Kaitlin. They seemed even more vengeful after they thought I was trying to take Claire's picture. *Probably for her weirdo gaming nerd channel,* they'd said. Among other, less flattering things.

They also made it very clear that if they ever caught me taking their picture again, I'd wish I had never been born. And, judging from the look in their eyes, they'd meant it. I was lucky I was able to walk away with my phone and my face intact. It probably helped that I was surrounded by people. Including . . .

"Hey!" someone calls from behind us.

I turn around and see Jacob jogging up the sidewalk.

"How's it going?" he asks.

"Okay," I say.

"Are you two filming again tonight?" he asks.

"Yup," Rochelle says. "Gonna see if we can trap those Twins. Though who knows, maybe we'll see a new ghost tonight. I hope."

"Sweet," he says. He looks to me and grins. "That was some sharp shooting today. You nearly got that ghost."

I shrug and feel a blush rise in my cheeks. I look to my feet.

"Yeah, if only Kaitlin hadn't knocked into me," I reply.

"Oh, well, you'll catch it next time."

There's an awkward silence as we walk together. Should I say something? Ask him a question?

"Well, um, good luck tonight," he finally says. "A few friends and I are going to get together to watch the stream. Can't wait! It feels like I know a celebrity."

A celebrity. He thinks I'm a celebrity. My head feels light with giddiness. So much so that I barely even notice him walk away.

"Oh no," Rochelle says.

"What?" I ask.

"Your head. It's getting so big, I don't think your headphones will fit anymore."

I give her a shove and she cackles.

I keep glancing over my shoulder, watching Jacob walk away.

He keeps looking over his shoulder, too.

×✗×

We hit our first snag the moment we walk in the front door. And by *snag*, I mean *impossible roadblock*.

"Sorry, girls," my dad says. "No streaming tonight."

"What?" I groan. "But *Dad*."

"Don't *but Dad* me," he says. "You two can do your homework together, but no streaming. Remember, Beatrice—school has to come first, and I don't want you two getting so sucked up in this that you lose your focus."

I open my mouth to mention the donations, but he cuts me off.

"*Even if* you're getting paid. I know you see this as a job, but you have the rest of your life to work a job. Right now, you need to focus on learning."

Frustration roars inside me, but Rochelle steps in before I can say something I'd regret.

"No worries, Mr. Robinson," she says. "We can hold off on streaming. We have plenty of time."

I glare at her, because we do *not* have plenty of time.

We only have until midnight Thursday before the game ends and we lose. But she's just smiling sweetly at my father, not even giving me a sideways glance. Which tells me she's up to something.

We head up to my bedroom, and when the door is closed and the books are out, her plan becomes clear.

"Okay," she says. "What are your thoughts on sneaking me in?"

"What?" I ask.

"Well, yeah," she says. "I can bike over and just hang out in the bushes and—"

I shake my head. "No way. If we get caught, my parents will trash all our streaming gear, no question."

She sighs. "It was worth a shot."

"Hopefully we can convince them to let you come over tomorrow," I say. "Or I could pack up the cameras and maybe go to yours? Though if they catch me outside of the house . . ."

She considers.

"Maybe," she says. "I guess we don't need full setup since we're going mobile anyway."

"Might be worth the risk," I say. "I doubt my parents will let you stay the night after yesterday."

"Okay," she says, nodding as she thinks it through. "I'll see what I can do. Tonight, though, maybe we can split-screen. I don't think it's a good idea to skip a day."

"Definitely not. The clock is ticking."

"And we can't upset our paid subscribers. They want content, and they paid for us to produce it. You know how fast the internet gets angry."

My phone vibrates. The moment I look to it, the screen lights up with a message I know all too well:

A GHOST IS NEAR

"Maybe we should pull it up quickly?" Rochelle says. "Get a few minutes in before—"

But there's a knock at the door before she finishes. It opens, and my dad pops his head in.

"How's work going?" he asks. He eyes our closed book bags, the lack of work on the bed.

"Um . . ."

"I'm just going to keep the door open," he says. "Get to work, you two."

He winces.

"Everything okay?" Rochelle asks.

He nods and sticks a finger in his mouth, looking confused.

"Yeah," he mumbles. "Just have a toothache. Strange, I just went to the dentist last week."

That makes me look up.

Not missing a tooth? You will be.

Before I can say anything, he turns and walks down the hall.

I think I might know where the Tooth Fairy hid last night . . .

23

I know I told Rochelle I'd wait until eleven before we tried split-screen filming.

That was the plan.

But my phone. Hasn't. Stopped. Ringing.

It started with a vibration. The normal notification, a flash of the screen saying a ghost was near.

That, I could ignore.

Then it started making noises.

Not the normal beeps or ringtones, no.

Chimes. Deep, resonant church chimes that nearly make me jump out of my skin the first time they ring.

On full volume.

At ten.

I scramble to turn the phone off and knock it to the floor in my haste. My bedroom is dark and my parents are *hopefully* still asleep. The phone skids underneath the bed and continues to toll loudly. I know my parents can hear. It's only a matter of time before they charge in and take my phone forever.

The phone screen is flashing under the bed, blinding me. I reach for it and manage to power it down.

I sit back on my feet, breathing and blinking rapidly, trying to get my vision to clear while I hope against hope that I don't hear my parents storming down the hall.

I strain my ears.

Blink away the afterglow of the flashing screen.

And that's when I see it.

Hiding under my bed.

A face.

A man's face.

His skin is shock white and his eyes black with white irises, his hair black and wiry.

He clings, upside down, to the bottom of my bed.

The moment I see him, he skitters away like a cockroach frightened by the sun.

I slap a hand to my mouth to keep from screaming and fumble for the light on my nightstand. The light clicks on, bathing the bedroom in a warm glow.

Slowly

ever

so

slowly

I bend back over and peer under the bed.

Nothing is there.

I stand on shaking legs and peer over the corner of my bed. But there's nothing on the far wall, nothing hiding in the shadows. I'm alone.

With a scared laugh, I flop down on my bed.

This can't be good. I'm either losing it or I'm actually *seeing* the ghosts. I mean, I thought they were real, but there's something even scarier about seeing them in real life.

I definitely hadn't seen that ghost in the game. I'd have remembered that crooked smile, those horrifying eyes . . .

I shake myself.

Glance at the clock beside my bed.

It's only ten thirty, but I know I can't wait around any longer. Knowing the ghost is in my room—and off camera—makes me feel more vulnerable than ever before. I have to capture it. It's the only way I'll know I'm safe.

But before I do, I have to make sure I'm getting this on camera. Everyone's expecting a show tonight, and I have to give it to them.

I creep downstairs as softly and quickly as I can.

Shadows scuttle around me, but I don't risk turning on the lights or turning on my phone. Every time I blink I fear I'll see whatever-it-was, the ghost I have no name for. I wish I had caught it on camera—then, I'd know what I was up against.

The moment my foot touches the bottom step, a light flickers on above me.

I yelp.

And there, in the living room, is my mother, arms crossed and a scowl on her face.

"And just what do you think you're doing sneaking around in the middle of the night?" she asks.

I try to look innocent.

"I was just, um, going to get a snack."

She rolls her eyes. "I wasn't born yesterday, Beatrice. I know you're about to go stream."

"I wasn't—"

"Be very careful what you say next. I know when you're lying. And you don't want to lie to me again."

"Okay," I say, defeated. I look to my feet. "I was going to stream. But you don't understand, Mom. We have so many followers now, and they're all *depending* on me." *You don't understand—I think the ghosts might be capable of hurting people for real.*

"I know it feels that way, honey," she replies, her voice oddly soft. "And I know how excited you are about all this. We're excited for you, too. Really. But you *have* to focus on school right now."

"But—"

"No buts," she says. "You need to sleep or your grades will start to slip. You and Rochelle can stream all you want on the weekend, or at a normal hour if your homework is done. No more of this sneaking around in the middle of the night, okay? Your father's already in enough pain. He doesn't need you making a racket."

I look to her. "What's wrong with Dad?"

"Toothache," she says. "But we'll take him to the dentist in the morning."

It's the Tooth Fairy. I know it is!

"Now," Mom continues, "it's bedtime." She holds out her hand. "Phone."

"What?"

She gives me a knowing look. "I know you can stream in your room," she says. Which is only sort of true, but still. She doesn't realize the danger she's in. If I don't play, if the ghosts continue to roam freely . . .

But I don't get a chance to try to change her mind.

The next moment, Dad begins to scream.

24

Mom and I race up the stairs.

Dad's screams are more like howls of pain, like a wounded animal, and I am torn between wanting to run toward him to help and running away so I don't have to see what has happened.

Because I know what has happened. Even though I'll never be able to say anything.

He's been attacked by a ghost.

We rush into the bathroom.

To see Dad standing by the sink in his pajamas.

His hands are to his face and he's staring at the mirror, his eyes wide.

Blood drips between his fingers.

"My toof!" he cries out in a muffled whine. "My toof if gone!"

Mom races over to him.

"We'll get you to urgent care," she says, concern clear on her face.

I feel my own blood rush from my head. I hate the sight of blood. It makes me woozy.

Makes me faint.

I sway.

The room sways, too.

Shifts to grayscale—just for a moment.

Just for a moment, everything gray and crackly, granular, coated with TV-screen static.

In the mirror, I see something dark congealing and throbbing in the corner above the shower curtain.

"Stay here," Mom says. Her voice slams me back, back into the too-bright bathroom with its too-red blood. "I'm going to take your father to the doctor. We'll be back soon."

She helps Dad out of the room. He keeps his hands to his mouth. I swear his wide eyes see nothing.

But I—

When they reach the stairs, I step over and rip back the shower curtain.

For the briefest second
      for less than a breath

I see darkness in the corner. A mass of shadowy black.

Shadow like oil, covered in white jags of stolen teeth, and in its long pincer, it holds my dad's tooth.

25

I follow Mom and Dad out of the bathroom and downstairs. I watch as they walk outside to the car, Dad leaning heavily against Mom. The moment they drive off, my phone is in my hands, and the **DARK[room]** app is open. But even though the entryway is filled with shadows, none of those shadows are filled with teeth. Nothing appears in the camera. The Tooth Fairy didn't follow us down here.

"Where are you?" I mutter. "I know you're here!"

It's not just fear that's fueling me now, though I'm definitely scared.

No, I'm angry. Angry that the ghosts would hurt someone I care about. Angry that they'd go after my father, when they've left me alone.

"Where are you!" I call out, so loud my voice startles even me.

My phone vibrates in response.

For a split second I consider heading back down

into the basement. Either grabbing the portable cam or just streaming down there. But I don't want to share this with the world. This ghost hurt my dad.

This is personal.

I follow the vibration, heading back toward the bathroom as the buzz grows louder and louder.

I know I should be scared, and I think part of me is. Goose bumps prickle over my skin, and my breath is fast and short. I'm alone in the house, and there is for sure an evil ghost that can hurt people, and all I'm armed with is a cell phone with an outdated camera and an app that seems to have unleashed all the ghosts in the first place. But it worked before with the Devouring Woman. It will work now.

I creep into the bathroom.

I try to ignore the blood in the sink and instead focus on the corners.

The shower curtain is pulled closed.

I know I left it open.

The moment my camera centers on the curtain, it begins to pulse and flicker rapidly.

It's here. It's here.

"I know you're in there," I say. My voice shakes.

So does my hand as I slowly reach out for the curtain

and draw

        it

                back.

In the camera's frame, darkness surges and roars in the shower, a growl so loud I scream out and nearly drop the phone as I stagger backward.

The darkness—the *Tooth Fairy*—unfolds itself, black rippling with jagged pearls of white as it grows, as it multiplies. Spreads to envelop the entire shower wall, and more. In a bubbling, gurgling, gnashing mass, the Tooth Fairy fills the shower. I know then what's happening.

It's growing because of the pain it caused my dad. Just like its description said: *Its sweet tooth is pain.*

"I won't let you hurt anyone else!" I yell out.

I steady the camera.

Try to find the Tooth Fairy's center.

The screen glows bright white. I've found it.

At that moment, a set of teeth sprout from the center, appearing like a beak of a jellyfish. They snap and dart forward, and with them come the pincers. They lash toward me, just like a jellyfish's arms. I tell myself that they can't hurt me, that it's just a game.

But when they smack me, I *feel* them.

The pincers knock me to the side.

Knock the phone from my hands.

I look to the shower, and although I can't see the Tooth Fairy without my phone, I know it's there. I can feel the coldness, the dread. And stranger still, I swear I see faint shadows curling along the tiles.

I drop to my knees and scramble toward the phone.

Something lashes against my back. I scream out in pain.

Another *something* knocks me to my chest and flips me over, pinning me to my back.

And now, it's no longer my imagination.

Without the phone

> I
>
> see
>
> the
>
> ghost.

It's *all* I can see.

A mass of roiling shadow and gnashing teeth that stretches over the entire bathroom. Its dozen tentacles pin me in place.

I stretch for my phone.

It's just out of reach.

The ghost roars. Its central mouth opens, and I can see my dad's bloody tooth in that maw, just as I can see the hundred other grinding, jagged teeth it stole from its other victims.

Two pincers stretch from its central mouth.

Tentacles press on my face, on my jaw.

Tentacles pry my mouth open.

The Tooth Fairy's growls become a laugh, deep and guttural. It's going to steal my teeth. All of them. And when it does, it will destroy me.

Tears stream from my eyes as the pincers snap and descend

> ever
>
> so
>
> slowly
>
>> toward my face.

Please no please no please no, I think on repeat.

I keep reaching for my phone. I can't even turn my head to see if I'm close, and my jaw hurts from the pressure of its tentacles. All I can see are the pincers. The stolen teeth.

A pincer reaches into my mouth.

I can taste it.

An electric, acrid, foul-egg taste that would make me throw up if I could.

Pain shoots through me as it grabs one of my molars

> and begins
>
> to
>
> TUG.

I cry out.

Scream.

Stretch.

No one is coming to save me. No one is home.

It tugs harder.

My fingers connect. Touch the cold phone.

I awkwardly grab it.

With my last remaining strength, I yank the phone up.

It vibrates wildly.

I don't even aim.

I hit the shutter button.

Light flashes.

The ghost screams.

And between one frantic breath and the next, the ghost is no more.

26

Silence fills the bathroom.

Silence so loud my ears ring.

All I hear is my breathing.

And then.

The phone pulses. An angry bee buzz.

I look down, and there, to my relief, three words flash on the screen.

TOOTH FAIRY CAPTURED

I reach in my mouth. All my teeth are still there, though one definitely hurts.

I reach to my back—my clothes haven't been ripped. There's no blood.

It's like the Tooth Fairy was never there at all.

Save for my dad. But he'll be okay. He'll be okay.

I caught the Tooth Fairy. Dad's safe now. We all are.

I'm so relieved I flop back on the tiles and stare up at the ceiling.

I breathe in and out, constantly flicking my tongue

over my teeth just to make sure they're all still there.

Then I raise my phone up.

"I'm done with you," I whisper.

I don't think twice.

I delete the **DARK[room]** app.

I'm done playing. If Rochelle's mad, fine. She can be mad. She'll get over it. We'll find a new game. Our loyal followers will remain loyal or they won't. It doesn't matter.

This game is dangerous.

I'm not going to play anymore, and I'm not going to let it play me.

27

I dream I am back in the hallway.

I know in my gut *which* hallway it is, even though I have no idea *where* it is. I know that I am in trouble.

Gritty gray darkness stretches before and behind me, pierced by shafts of moonlight that seem not to illuminate but rather cut through the dark. The walls are rough wood, the windows jagged glass. Cobwebs stretch like rafters overhead, and my feet creak menacingly on the splinter-filled floor.

Something stirs at the end of the hall. A shadow, bleeding from the edges.

It's her.

I don't want to see.

I turn.

I run.

The hall stretches farther with every step. Cold creeps over my skin as I run. A cold that makes my breath come out in clouds and ice to rime the broken windows.

I run faster.

Tears fall down my face, freezing on my cheeks before they hit the floor. Behind me, I hear her voice.

"You cannot run from us, Beatrice," she rasps. Her voice is silken and harsh at the same time, like an old recording of a beautiful singer. *"You are already ours."*

The hall forks.

Shadows congeal in front of me.

But it isn't the bound woman.

It's a man.

I think it's a man.

He towers in the hall, stooped so his head won't touch the ceiling. Hair hangs lank around his head, his clothes are a dark smear smock. And his hands . . .

He holds his hands in front of him, his fingers pointing to the ground. And on each fingertip is a long, needlelike nail that touches the floor. Where the nails touch wood, smoke hisses up. He smiles, his teeth blinding, his eyes wide and burning white.

I run down the other hall.

Behind me, the terrifying man laughs while the ghost woman calls out.

Above me, something scuttles spiderlike on the ceiling.

It races in front of me.

Darts down a wall.

Forces me to stop.

It looks like a spider.

Four shadowy limbs.

Bulbous black body.

But its face is shock white, skeletal. A *skull*. It smiles, its teeth breaking and grinding.

"*You have caught two of us,*" it says. "*But we have already caught* you."

I try to turn, to run, but thousands of black threads snare around me, stretching to the shadows of the walls, binding me in place in an intricate spiderweb. The creature before me scuttles up a strand. As it nears, its skull jaw opens and splits, becomes two piercing fang mandibles.

I scream.

I struggle.

I don't wake up.

"*Do you not enjoy our game, Beatrice?*" comes the woman's voice.

A hand on my face.

She turns me to face her, the threads giving just enough for that motion, but not enough to set me free.

The beautiful ghost woman.

Moonlight illuminates half of her face. What is in moonlight is beautiful, her skin smooth, her eyes ageless. But the dark reveals her monstrous nature—the sunken cheeks, the skeleton beneath.

Behind her towers the long-fingered man. The hall seems to breathe and bend around him.

"*You wanted to play,*" she says. She sounds almost sad. "*You can't give up now. We won't let you. Our games have only just begun. You've already brought us one new toy. You will bring us more.*"

At her feet appear the two Twins. They smile up at me.

She caresses my face. Her fingers freeze and burn like frostbite. I can't wince away. "*You will make a delightful spirit,*" she whispers as she assesses me. She smiles. "*Two days, Beatrice. And then, you are mine.*"

Her grip tightens.

Pain explodes.

I don't wake up.

I don't wake up.

WEDNESDAY
Day Six

28

"You look like dog poop," Rochelle says.

"Thanks," I mutter. "Happy Wednesday to you, too."

"What's wrong?" she asks. We sit outside the school, thirty minutes before classes start. I'd texted her the moment I woke up, telling her to meet me early.

She needs to know I'm done. No matter what she—or the ghost woman from my dreams—says, I'm done.

"I'm not playing anymore," I declare.

"Ha-ha, very funny," she says. "But it's not April Fools'. We just got another two hundred followers last night. *And* a few more donations. We can't quit now. I'm already all geared up for the next stream—I think I'm going to pretend to get attacked, maybe find some fake blood, what do you think?"

The thought of fake blood just reminds me of my dad standing over the bathroom sink. I force the images down. He and Mom came back late last night. Nobody could explain how his tooth had just fallen out, and they couldn't find it in the bathroom when they looked. Dad's still in some pain, but not as much as before.

"*I* can quit," I say. "And I am."

She raises an eyebrow. "Is this another trick?" she asks. "Like, you're going to say you're quitting but then, I don't know, some ghost magically shows up and forces you to finish? We only have until tomorrow night, Bea!"

I'm about to speak up when her eyes flick over my shoulder. She groans.

"What's up?" someone asks behind me.

Jacob.

"Beatrice here was just telling me about how she was going to stop playing **DARK[room]**," Rochelle says.

"What?" Jacob asks. "Why? What happened?"

My heart does a little flip when he asks that. *What happened?* As if he might actually believe that the game was more than a game. As if he might guess the truth.

For a moment I consider just saying nothing, trying to change the subject. Jacob and I haven't talked—really talked—since we were little kids. But I used to trust him, and I need *someone* to believe me.

"The ghosts are real," I say.

Rochelle rolls her eyes and mutters, *"Not this again"* right as Jacob whispers, *"I knew it."*

"I—"

"Look," Rochelle interrupts, "if you're scared, it's okay, you can admit it. But it's just a game, Bea. It can't hurt you."

"It *did* hurt me!" I yell out. Jacob actually jumps, and a few kids look over. I lower my voice. "Look, Rochelle, I know you think I'm making this all up for, I don't know, a good performance or whatever. I'm not. Last night . . ." I swallow and look to Jacob. Unlike Rochelle, he watches me like he believes every word. "Last night my dad got hurt. One of the ghosts . . . the Tooth Fairy. It came for him. It stole one of his teeth. Then the ghost tried to steal mine."

The moment I say it I flash back to seeing him, shocked and bleeding in the bathroom. The terrifying Tooth Fairy expanding as my dad's tooth gave it power . . .

"Oh no," Jacob whispers. "Is he okay?"

"He's fine," I say. "They went to the ER, but he's fine. It's why I didn't sleep much last night; I was up waiting for them to get home."

Rochelle is watching me. Her gaze isn't exactly disbelieving. It's more calculated. Calculating. Like she's trying to catch me in a lie.

"You can call him if you want," I say. "I'm telling the truth."

"I'm sure you are," Rochelle says slowly. "But, I don't know, Bea. You really want me to believe it was a ghost that did it? He probably just, like, chipped a tooth in his sleep. Happens all the time. My mom lost a crown that way, and it wasn't—"

"It was the ghost, Rochelle!" I say. "What do I have to tell you to make you believe me? A ghost attacked my dad and I'm not playing anymore. I caught the Tooth Fairy and I deleted the app and I'm done."

"Wait," she says. "You caught the Tooth Fairy?"

"Yes," I say, even though that's not the important part. The important part is that I'm done. "I couldn't let it hurt anyone again."

"Why didn't you call me?" she asks. "We could have split-screened or something. You should have filmed it."

"I—what—" I stammer. *"This isn't a game anymore,"* I manage.

I pull out my phone. Jacob watches this all silently.

"Look," I say. "I deleted the app. It's gone. I'm done. If you want to play, fine. But you're going to do it without me."

"The developers went dark, remember?" she says. "You might have had the last copy. I can't believe you'd delete it, Bea. That's so selfish. We were just about to be famous. We were about to be *rich*."

"Don't you get it?" I ask. "It's hurting people, Rochelle. It hurt my dad. Who knows who's going to be next?"

"It's just. A. Game," she says. She looks at my phone. Her expression changes, becomes angry. "And you know, the next time you try to lie to me, you could at least try to cover your tracks better. Come on, Bea. This is novice stuff."

Without another word, she stands and walks away.

I sit there, stunned, and watch her go. Only after a few moments do I remember Jacob is still standing there awkwardly. He clears his throat.

"I believe you," he admits.

He says it so quietly I almost don't hear him.

"What?" I ask.

He sits down beside me.

"I believe you," he says. "About the ghosts. I guess . . . I've always believed in the supernatural, you know? And when I heard you were playing **DARK[room]**, I did some research. I found those message boards. I don't think they were a hoax or social marketing. I think they might have been real."

I don't know what's worse: the fact that Rochelle still doesn't believe me or the fact that Jacob does.

"What am I going to do?" I ask.

"Play," he says. "Honestly, the only way to get through it is probably to win."

"But I can't. You heard me before, and I meant it. I'm not playing anymore. Besides, I deleted it last night. I'm not going to risk it."

He looks down to the phone I still hold in my hands.

"It looks like the game doesn't agree."

"What?" I ask. "What do you—"

I look down at my phone.

The home screen is still lit up.

And there, impossibly, the **DARK[room]** app waits.

29

I'm jumpy all morning.

I swear, every time I walk down the hall between classes, I see glimpses of the Twins darting between people's legs.

Every time I open my locker, I expect to see some new, terrifying ghost peering out.

I keep my phone in my locker, muffled beneath a pile of clothes just in case it starts to make noise. I can't risk it.

I can't play anymore.

But when I get to gym class, I quickly realize the game isn't done playing with me.

"What did you do to her?"

I barely realize who's talking before Kaitlin shoves me against a locker.

"Who?" I manage to get out. Kaitlin holds me against a changing room locker.

"Claire!" she says. She glowers at me. The other girls in the locker room pretend we aren't there at all.

So much for fame meaning I was safe from bullies. "What did you do?"

"I have no clue what you're talking about," I say. "I don't even know her."

"You were taking her picture yesterday with all those other *freaks*," she retorts. "What did you do? Put it online so someone could kidnap her?"

Her accusations make my heart race. Not because I'm worried about what she might do to me—I'm terrified because the last time I saw Claire, the ghost Twins were near her.

What if *they* attacked her?

"What do you mean, kidnap?" I ask. "Is she missing?"

Kaitlin shakes her head. Her eyes are wide. Wild. Desperate.

"She stopped texting me last night," she says. She drops her hands and steps back. Suddenly, without her anger, she looks lost and scared. "I went by her place this morning because I usually give her a ride, but she wasn't home. Her parents thought she left early to walk to school because they didn't hear her get up, but she was definitely there after dinner. Something happened to her. I know it." Her eyes refocus on me. "What did you do to her?"

I think of the Twins. The ghost woman's words:

You've already brought us a new toy. You will bring us more.

What have I done?

"Nothing," I say out loud. "Honestly, I don't know what happened to her. I wasn't trying to take a picture of her yesterday, I swear. It was just for a game."

"You were taking pictures of her for a game?"

"What? No, you don't understand, it's like this augmented reality—"

She puts up her hand. "You know what? I don't care. Just stay away from me, freak." She walks away, toward her locker, and calls out over her shoulder. "And you better *hope* Claire comes back, or else you'll be the next one to go missing."

xXx

I can't get Kaitlin's warning out of my head all during gym class.

I can't stop wondering what happened to Claire. I try to convince myself it has nothing to do with me, but I know that's not the case.

We practice laps and treading water, and I go through the motions on autopilot. I never thought I'd be thankful that the pool is so cold—it makes me focus on the here and now, on each breath and stroke.

It takes all my concentration to keep myself from shivering.

Near the end of class, I realize it isn't just the pool that's making goose bumps break out over my skin. When our coach blows the whistle and says it's time to get changed, I realize that something is wrong. Something is very wrong.

The pool is getting colder.

Most of my classmates are already out of the pool and drying off. Kaitlin is still in the water with me.

And then I feel it.

A cold current of electricity, a buzz that hums in my bones just like the phone had vibrated in my hands. I feel my blood pulsing through my veins, every thud getting faster, stronger, my heart panicking as dread washes over me:

A ghost is near.

And I don't have my phone to defend myself.

I can't even see it.

But . . . wait.

No.

There, at the far edge of the pool . . .

I blink.

I swear I see something under the water. Billowing and black, like a cape made of shadows, like an octopus with a thousand thin tentacles.

It's heading straight toward Kaitlin.

I gasp and kick my way over to her, but it feels like I'm swimming through gelatin.

Kaitlin swims slowly over to the side of the pool, talking with some of her friends, completely oblivious to the shadow swimming closer to her.

I try to call out. Honestly I try to call out, but every time I open my mouth to scream, water splashes in, leaving me spluttering and gasping.

The shadow nears her.

And as it nears, I see what it truly is.

A woman.

Her head slips above the water's surface, only inches away from Kaitlin. The ghost's eyes are white moons, her skin gray like ash, her hair black and billowing out around her in impossibly long strands.

Strands that twist and curl in the water around them. Like eels.

The ghost woman turns her head to me
and smiles.

Her gray lips reveal sharp white teeth.

"Kaitlin!" I manage to yell out, before another burst of water makes me choke.

Kaitlin is at the ladder, her hands on the railings, a foot on a rung.

She looks to me.

And fast as a snake, tendrils of black hair snap from the water, wrapping around Kaitlin's wrists and ankles.

She doesn't even have a chance to scream before she's dragged underwater.

30

The moment Kaitlin disappears underwater, the strange slowness in the world disappears.

I don't think. I react.

I dive under and swim with all my might toward the swarming mass of black hair and thrashing limbs in front of me. Kaitlin looks like she's enveloped in a cocoon of black threads, her arms and legs kicking against the ghost that drags her under. She thrashes and writhes, but the ghost woman is too strong. I can barely see the ghost, just the occasional flash of her white dress, the briefest glimpse of her dead white eyes.

With every inch closer, the pool around me changes.

Color fades away, blue blurring to white and gray, a film-screen crackle that hisses in my ears, like I'm viewing it all through the game's camera lens.

I swim harder, pushing against the burn in my lungs, because with every stroke, Kaitlin and the ghost get farther down, always just out of reach, as the pool yawns open below us, stretching down, down into an endless void that makes my chest lurch with vertigo.

I know if the ghost drags Kaitlin down there, she'll never come back up.

Pain screams in my lungs. I'm running out of air.

I have to help her.

Even though she's a bully, I can't let her get hurt, not like this, not when it's my fault.

I close in.

Her hand stretches out through the churning black swarm of strands, and I grab it and yank and swim upward with all my might.

The water's surface is impossibly far away.

I don't think I can make.

I don't think—

    The ghost woman appears in front of me.

The little air in my lungs escapes as I scream out. Her white eyes are wide, her mouth set in a snarl. Black hair haloes her, even as strands still desperately drag Kaitlin down into the depths.

"*Let her drown and I will let you go,*" she growls in my ear. "*She would never rescue you.*"

Hair curls dangerously by my kicking legs. I know the ghost will follow through on her threat, just as I know she is telling the truth. Kaitlin would happily let me drown.

For a split second I consider it.

Claire is already gone. If Kaitlin disappears, there won't be anyone in the school who bullies me anymore.

The ghost woman smiles wide, sharp teeth shark-like, and in the whites of her eyes, I see it:

I see myself walking down the hall, smiling and talking to everyone I pass. Everyone is excited to see me. They've all been tuning into the stream, and Rochelle and I have become local celebrities. Even the teachers seem extra warm, waving at me from the classrooms and saying how excited they are for the next game.

"*Your life would be better off without her,*" the ghost woman whispers. "*Let her go . . . Let her go.*"

I shake my head, and the oppressive weight of water crashes back around me. Tendrils of hair snag my ankles and wrists, dragging me down into the impossible void below.

The void into which Kaitlin is also plummeting.

I grab ahold of Kaitlin's outstretched hand. I don't care what visions the ghost shows me. I'm not going to let someone get hurt. Not even Kaitlin.

"*You'll both drown if you try to save her!*" the ghost howls in my head. She swims savagely beside us, trying to yank us under. But I kick and swim harder than I ever have.

The surface is so far away. My breath is almost gone. Black spots dance in my vision.

Below us, the void beckons.

But then something new appears above. A splash. A ripple. And as I feel my breath leave me, a strong hand grabs my wrist and pulls me up, pulls me free of the ghost woman's hair.

In seconds I'm sputtering and gasping on the edge of the pool. My vision swims, my limbs shake. I see the bleary outlines of my classmates looking down on Kaitlin and me with concern while the teacher yells to give us room, to get the nurse.

He leans over me, pats the side of my face.

"Beatrice," our teacher says, "can you hear me?"

Over his shoulder, the dripping form of the ghost woman appears.

Fear and exhaustion finally get the best of me, and I pass out.

×✗×

No one knows what happened in the pool except me.

Not even Kaitlin remembers.

I ask her what happened when I finally came to in the nurse's office. She says she was on the ladder and slipped, and the next thing she knew, I was dragging her down. Nothing about a ghost of billowing hair.

Nothing about nearly being dragged down into an endless expanse.

In fact, she seems to think *I* attacked *her*.

By the time school is over, rumors have exploded across campus. People whisper as I pass, saying that I've become unhinged, that I tried to drown Kaitlin out of jealousy. Others say I was trying to save her, though there are only a few taking my side. Everyone wants drama, and what better story is there than a rivalry gone wrong?

No one else saw the ghost. Not a single one of my classmates saw anything other than Kaitlin slipping off the ladder. From there, the accounts vary. Some say I was right beside her and pulled her in. Others say I raced over to try to help her but nearly drowned myself. Everyone in that pool saw something a little different. There is only one consensus: We would have both drowned if Coach Vaughn hadn't saved us.

It makes me feel very, very alone.

While I wait at my locker for Rochelle to show, I reach in and pull out my phone.

The battery is nearly dead.

DARK[room] is still running.

I glance around quickly, but no one is looking at me. I open the game and pull up the ghost dictionary.

I want to know which ghost I saw in the pool. I want to know what I'm up against.

1. ~~DEVOURING WOMAN~~
2. THE TWINS
3. ~~TOOTH FAIRY~~
4. XXX
5. XXX
6. XXX
7. XXX

I grumble with frustration.

Even though I've seen more than those three ghosts, there's no information. I bet I have to take a photo of them for their details to come up. Great.

I click on the Twins.

THE TWINS MAY LOOK INNOCENT. BUT WE ASSURE YOU, THEY'RE NOT. THEY LOVE TO PLAY GAMES. BUT THERE'S ALWAYS ONE OUTCOME: THEY WIN. YOU DIE.

They love to play games.

If they're anything like what that creepy pool ghost did to Kaitlin, I can't imagine Claire is having any fun.

"I hear you tried to drown Kaitlin," Rochelle says.

Her voice makes me jump.

"I didn't," I say quickly. "I can't believe you'd actually believe that."

She rolls her eyes. "I don't," she says. "Just like I don't believe you're done playing **DARK[room]**."

"I—"

"You're literally playing it right now," she says.

I look down at my phone and hastily exit the app before pocketing my phone.

"I wasn't," I say. "I was researching. Rochelle . . . I know you don't believe me, but Kaitlin was attacked in the pool. There was a ghost. She had long black hair that was trying to drag us both down and drown us."

Rochelle raises an eyebrow. "A ghost with long black hair? C'mon, Beatrice. You can do better than that. That's so cliché."

"It's what I saw!"

"Underwater," she says. "Unless you're taking your phone swimming, I don't believe you."

"That's what I've been trying to tell you!" I say. "I can see the ghosts in real life now! They're getting worse. They're getting dangerous."

She sighs in frustration.

"Save it for the stream, girl," she says. "Speaking of, are we playing tonight or not?"

"I—"

"And don't give me any more lies about being done. I know you want this as much as I do. Just make sure to save your stories for when we're recording, okay? You don't need to convince me the ghosts are real—save that for the audience. Hey—I bet if you told everyone tonight that you saved Kaitlin from a ghost, we'd get a ton more donations. What do you think?"

But I'm not listening to her. Not really.

My phone has begun to buzz. I know that pulse too well.

A ghost is near.

The trouble is, I don't need my phone to tell me that.

I can see him.

31

Rochelle notices my expression.

"What is it?" she asks. She turns around.

I fully expect her to scream. After all, that's what I want to do, but the fear is lodged in my throat. I can't scream or move or do anything I know I should be doing right now, because I also know that this should be impossible.

The hall is nearly empty of kids. But the few who remain don't seem to notice the creature that scuttles above them on the ceiling. It's a few doors away, but I can already make out its broken limbs, its skull-white face. As it nears, I realize it isn't a spider at all—it's a human, with his arms and legs broken and bent so they look like spider limbs. The clicking of its joints fills my ears, but when Rochelle stares down the hall, she apparently sees nothing.

"What?" she asks again.

"There's a ghost," I whisper.

Rochelle rolls her eyes.

"We're not on camera," Rochelle says. "You can drop the act."

"It's not an act," I insist. "It's getting closer. The man with the broken limbs. He's on the ceiling."

Rochelle stares straight at the ghost that gets closer with every breath. She doesn't see a thing.

Finally, I'm able to get my limbs to function. I pull out my phone and raise it in front of both of us so she can see the creature.

Its name comes up onscreen.

THE BROKEN MAN

"What is that?" Rochelle asks as the twisted thing nears.

I don't answer.

Instead, when the camera centers, I take its picture.

Light flashes, the camera shakes. A scream rips through the hall and at first I don't know if it's the ghost or Rochelle. The creature darts away, scuttling across the ceiling faster than I can follow.

"Careful!" Rochelle yells. And for a split second, I think she's actually worried. Think that she is finally believing that this is real, that I'm not just playing. But then she pulls out her phone and starts recording. "I don't want to miss you capturing this one. It's too creepy!"

I nearly drop my phone in disbelief.

But she isn't paying attention to me. She grabs my arm and starts pulling me down the hall, in the direction the Broken Man went.

"What are you doing?" I ask.

"We have to capture it!" she replies. She zooms her phone in on me. "That's right, fans, your daring hosts, Butterfly and Crimson, are dashing off to fight another ghost. This terrifying creature is called the Broken Man, and we can only imagine what terrors it holds for us. Especially since, just this afternoon, Crimson rescued one of our classmates from *another* ghost."

She flips the camera around to film herself.

"You heard it here first, ghosts and ghouls—DARK[room] isn't just a game. It's released *actual* ghosts into the world, and if we don't find and capture them soon—"

"This isn't a game anymore!" I say. I yank my hand away. "Stop it, Rochelle. Just stop filming. This isn't funny. This isn't a game. Kaitlin was nearly killed, and who knows what happened to Claire. My dad was injured. This isn't fun anymore."

But rather than take my words seriously, Rochelle—who has turned the camera back to me—is nodding enthusiastically.

166

Clearly, she wants to get my protests on camera.

Clearly, she thinks—or knows—it will get us more viewers.

I growl in frustration. Nothing I can say or do will convince her, unless she sees the ghosts for herself. And if she does, it may be too late.

"What's going on?" someone calls.

I look over and see Jacob.

Great. Even more of an audience.

He jogs down the hall to catch up to us.

"We're on the trail of another ghost," Rochelle says. "And Crimson here is worried it's going to hurt someone if we aren't fast, so we better get going! You in?"

Jacob nods. But he isn't nearly as enthusiastic as Rochelle. He watches me warily.

"What ghost is it?" he asks.

I hold up my phone and open the ghost glossary.

THE BROKEN MAN

HIS BODY ISN'T THE ONLY BROKEN THING.
HE CAN BREAK THE WORLD AROUND YOU.
SHOW YOU GLIMPSES OF THE
NETHERWORLD.
AND IF HE CATCHES YOU,
HE'LL DRAG YOU THERE.
FOREVER.

"The Netherworld?" Jacob asks. "Like the underworld?"

Rochelle is already walking ahead of us. "Sure," she calls over her shoulder. "Ghosts gotta come from somewhere, right? Hurry up, Crimson. We need your phone."

I look to Jacob. And I try to make myself look as serious as I can.

"I don't want to do this," I whisper. "She doesn't understand. This is real. No matter what I say, she won't believe me."

He swallows, looks to Rochelle.

"I know," he replies. "But I do. Which is why we need to follow her. And protect her." He puts a hand on my shoulder. "Don't worry, we'll keep her safe and beat the game and then it's all over."

First we have to beat the game, I think.

I don't tell him that. I don't want to let him know what I really think: We can't beat this game.

It's already won.

32

We follow Rochelle down the hall. I find it ridiculous that she's the one in the lead when she can't even see the ghost, but it's clear she doesn't care. This is action. This is what the viewers want to see, and she is living for it.

"Can you see it?" she calls out. Once more, I am shocked that there aren't any teachers out, demanding to know why kids are running through the halls. We pass a few other students, but no one really looks at us twice.

I look through the camera.

"There!" I reply, pointing toward the biology lab.

The three of us head into the empty classroom.

The door clicks shut behind us, and the sudden silence and shadows are menacing.

"Does it feel colder in here to you?" Jacob asks.

I nod. Goose bumps have broken out over my skin, and there's an electricity in the air that I know isn't all nerves. The shades are drawn, and the room is darker than it should be; shadows lie thick over the long tables and shelves. Static crackles from my phone's speakers.

"It's definitely in here," Rochelle says. Her eyes are wide and excited.

I swing the camera around. It vibrates steadily, and the room through the lens is nightmarish and still.

"Nothing," I say.

"Maybe it's hiding under the tables," Rochelle suggests. She grins and drops to her knees.

The phone vibrates stronger.

"I think she's right," I whisper, and drop down beside her.

I keep the phone up, scanning beneath the tables in front of us. Shadows lurk like spiderwebs, thicker than they should be.

The vibration gets stronger.

"It's getting closer," I say.

Jacob is at my side. A second later, his hand grabs my arm. Hard.

"Beatrice?" he whispers, his voice shaking.

"Yeah?"

"I think . . . I think it's behind us."

I turn around and look where Jacob is staring.

I don't even have to bring up my phone.

The Broken Man hangs from the table behind us, his broken-jaw face jeering. He doesn't move, and that seems even more dangerous. He's inspecting us.

Rochelle turns around.

"I don't see anything," she whispers.

And she shouldn't be able to see anything. Neither should Jacob. So why can he and I see the ghost only feet away from our faces?

Hands trembling, I slowly raise the camera.

"Bea?" Rochelle asks. And now she actually sounds a little worried. Like Jacob maybe seeing things makes this more real to her. "Bea, what's there?"

I don't answer.

My phone buzzes rapidly.

A hissing, clicking noise comes from the Broken Man as his mandible-like jaws rattle and his head twists all the way around.

I center the phone.

The screen glows blue.

And right before I take the shot, the Broken Man launches himself at Rochelle.

Rochelle cries out as the ghost slams into her, skidding her backward across the floor.

"Rochelle!" Jacob and I yell at the same time.

We both scramble over to her, but the ghost is terrifyingly fast. Even without the phone raised, I see thick black threads shoot from his jaw, wrapping around her in a cocoon.

"What's happening to me?" she yells in fear as her

arms snap close to her body. As the ghost binds her tighter.

Jacob reaches her side before I do, but the ghost swats him away with a twisted limb. Jacob goes sliding.

He doesn't get up.

I raise the phone.

"Beatrice?!" Rochelle yells, eyes wide. "What's—"

Black threads twist around her mouth, binding her silent.

Her eyes widen.

The ghost lowers himself over her, his mandibles opening wide and that horrible rattling hiss growing louder.

Blue light glows in the sockets of his skull eyes.

That blue light reflects in Rochelle's terrified stare.

I center the ghost.

The camera glows.

I take a photo.

Light flashes. The camera pulses. I can't see.

There is no sound. No scream of a captured ghost. No struggling thuds.

It takes my eyes far too long to readjust in the unearthly darkness.

Finally, I see.

My heart drops.

The ghost is gone.

So, too, is Rochelle.

33

"Rochelle?!" I yell out.

I scramble over to where she was just standing, leaving the phone behind.

I keep calling her name, over and over.

As if she might be hiding from me.

As if it might be that easy.

But deep down I know the truth.

She is gone.

Just like Claire, she is gone.

And it's all my fault.

Tears fill my eyes as I scramble about, looking everywhere for my missing friend.

Someone puts a hand on my shoulder and my heart leaps with hope and fear—hope it's her, fear it's another ghost. But when I turn around, I see Jacob. Just Jacob. And he looks just as lost as I feel.

"What happened?" he asks.

"I don't—I don't know," I reply.

He shakes his head as if trying to shake out of a daze. "Where's Rochelle?" he asks.

"I don't—"

"I saw it," he whispers, clearly shocked. "I saw a ghost, Bea. How did I see a ghost?"

"Because they're real," I reply. "They're real, and I think they took Rochelle."

He doesn't say anything for a few moments. He looks around the dark biology lab. He looks at me.

Then he looks at my phone, still on the floor behind me. The screen is facedown.

"Maybe—" he whispers. Then he makes a move toward it.

"Don't!" I yell out. "It's dangerous."

He pauses.

"I know," he says. "But maybe it has a clue. Maybe it's the only way to end this."

"I . . . okay," I relent.

He goes over and picks up the phone. I don't move a muscle. I keep staring about, expecting to see the ghost again, hoping to see Rochelle step out of the shadows with her camera raised and a goofy grin on her face. *Gotcha, guys! This will be so good for the stream.*

She doesn't appear. This isn't one of her pranks.

Jacob picks up the phone and looks at the screen. His eyebrows are furrowed, his eyes reflecting in the screen's glare.

"Well?" I ask.

He pokes it a few times.

"Well, I think there's some good news."

He shuffles over to me and holds out the phone.

1. ~~DEVOURING WOMAN~~
2. THE TWINS
3. ~~TOOTH FAIRY~~
4. XXX
5. ~~THE BROKEN MAN~~
6. XXX
7. XXX

"Looks like you caught it," he says.

I stare blankly at the phone. I don't reach for it. I don't ever want to touch it again.

"Then where did she go?" I ask.

He examines the phone. Taps the Broken Man's bio and reads it to himself.

"The Netherworld?" he whispers.

I stare at him.

"What?" he asks. "You make it seem like that's harder to believe than a *video game* releasing real ghosts. Pretty much every culture around the world has some mention of an underworld—what if this game managed to tap into that?"

"I just . . . I don't want to believe it. Because if she's in the Netherworld, how are we supposed to get her back?"

"I don't know," he replies.

34

I vaguely remember walking home alone, even though Jacob is insistent that we stick together. I tell him I'll be fine, that I have the phone, that my parents won't let him inside anyway.

At least, I think I walk home alone.

Every once in a while I swear I catch a glimpse of a tiny figure dashing out of sight behind bushes. The Twins, following me.

Well, let them follow. I don't care.

I can't care about anything besides rescuing Rochelle.

I eat dinner with Mom and Dad and can't even focus on anything they say or anything we eat, which makes me feel bad since Dad is still in pain after the Tooth Fairy stole his molar.

Another person I care about, hurt because of me.

I don't talk all through dinner. All I want to do is talk about Rochelle, and what would I say? My parents will never believe me if I tell them what happened.

They'll think I've lost it. Worse—they might call Rochelle's parents, and then what will happen? Rochelle didn't come home tonight. They have to be worried.

I wonder if Jacob's said anything to them. But what can he say? He probably just lied and said she came over to mine.

I don't eat. I just poke at my plate and think about Rochelle, and our stream, and how none of this would have happened if it hadn't been for me.

I don't even flinch when I see shapes at the corners of my vision. I don't look to see the Twins watching me, even though I know they're there. I can hear them giggling, even if my parents can't.

I'm in such a funk that when Mom gently suggests I take a bath to relax, I don't fight it. I even let her draw one for me.

Which is how I find myself surrounded by bubbles in a candlelit bath.

It should be relaxing, except for the fact that I can't relax. I can't *let* myself relax.

I lie in the tub, neck-deep in lavender-scented bubbles, and all I can do is stare at my phone.

I refuse to look at **DARK[room]**. And I manage, too . . . for at least two minutes. Then I give in, for a split second. I pull up the app and look around the bathroom, checking for ghosts.

Though if I'm being honest, what I'm really hoping to see is Rochelle.

If Jacob's right and she was dragged to the Netherworld, then maybe the app will let me see that world. Or, if nothing else, maybe if I'm able to beat the game tonight, I can get her back.

But there's nothing in the bathroom. No hint of a ghost, no hint of Rochelle. Not the slightest vibration, not the slightest crackle. I can't win if the ghosts don't show up. I can't win if they aren't willing to play. And right now, they know that the best way to torture me is to stay away. I can't do anything.

So instead I pull up my camera roll and skim through the photos, starting from the most recent and going back through time.

It goes back years. Tears form at the corners of my eyes as I flick backward.

Hundreds of impromptu selfies. Blurry shots of us riding bikes or on hikes. Sleepovers. Trying out different makeup tutorials. A few hundred photos from some local anime conventions, her and me dressed as our favorite characters in costumes we'd spent weeks sewing. That was before we'd gotten really into gaming and streaming, back when our true love was watching anime and reading manga.

I really, really wish we'd never grown out of

that phase, that we'd never fallen in love with video games.

If we hadn't, she'd still be here. She'd still be safe.

I sniff and wipe away a tear with a bubbly arm, my vision blurring for a second.

But, wait—

My vision isn't blurring.

There's something wrong with the photo.

It's a photo of the two of us by the lake from last summer. I'm in focus. So is the scenery. But Rochelle is blurry.

How . . . ?

I swipe to the next photo. Still on the beach, a slightly different pose. Once more, I'm in focus, and she is blurred out.

I keep scrolling back.

She's blurry. In every

single

photo.

"No," I whisper, swiping faster.

In every photo, she fades out more and more. Blurring like ink dropped into water, her image spreading and fading until . . .

Until . . .

I pause, my breath caught in my throat.

I know this selfie.

It's her and me at a restaurant, sitting in the same booth. In the picture, I'm laughing my head off because she got ketchup all over her face. It's one of my favorite photos of us because it was right after a convention and we were still in costume and we were both so completely exhausted that everything felt more hilarious than it really was.

In the picture, I look tired and happy, my head thrown back and my arm looped around her shoulders.

Except my arm is hovering over empty space.

There's no blur. No faded image.

Rochelle isn't there at all.

But in the booth behind us is a different face. A face that I know wasn't there before.

The ghost woman from my dreams. The shape-shifting monstrosity, dressed in white robes and bound with rope. She is in the photo, right behind where Rochelle *should* be.

And she is smiling.

35

I skim through the rest of the photos.

In every shot of Rochelle and me, Rochelle is missing.

As if she was never there at all.

As if the ghosts haven't just taken her, they're removing her from my life. From my history.

I know if I don't win, she'll be removed from my future as well.

I almost text Jacob to see how he's doing, to see what sort of cover he's told his parents, to see if his photos of her are also blank. But I don't want to worry him more. Rochelle may be like a sister to me, but she's *actually* his sister—it must be horrible to feel so helpless. At least I have the option of playing the game.

My only weapon against the ghosts is also the only reason they're attacking in the first place.

Ugh. I should get out and dry off. Maybe try to play for a few minutes, just to see if anything's around.

Besides, the water is starting to get cold.

Actually . . .

The water isn't just a little cold. The moment I realize it's cooling off, I realize it's cooling off *quickly*. Within moments, the bathwater is frigid, like ice water.

And the steam on the mirror is starting to crystallize.

I gasp from fear and cold and drop the phone to the bath mat, quickly getting out of the tub and wrapping a towel around me. And then another.

My breath comes out in puffs.

The candles flicker.

In the mirror, something moves.

I freeze.

Her body is a blur in the frosted glass, but I know who—what—she is.

The tattered white dress.

The graying skin.

The black hair that curls and twists like venomous serpents.

I turn slowly, my breath pounding my lungs.

She rises from the bathtub, water drip-drip-dripping from her gnarled fingers and sodden hair, though her dress billows like she's under the waves. Her face is obscured by black strands.

Between us, my phone still lies on the bath mat.

I stare at it.

Stare at her.
Tense
seconds
tick
by.

And then, before she can attack, I lunge forward to grab the phone.

She is faster.

Her hair snaps around my outstretched wrists. My fingers tense, only inches from the phone. I growl and try to reach, but no matter how hard I struggle, she doesn't budge.

Instead, she floats out of the bathtub and lowers herself in front of me.

I try to look away, try to keep focused on the phone only just outside my grasp. But a strand of her hair twists in front of my chin and forces my gaze up.

Her face is only inches from mine.

And her face is terrifying.

Because it isn't the ghost woman I saw before.

Not anymore.

She looks like Rochelle.

36

"Look what you did," her gravelly voice growls. "Look what you did to me."

"I . . . I didn't . . ."

I can't look away.

Rochelle's dark skin has gone pallid, her usual braids undone and sinuous, her brilliant eyes dull, and her once-easy smile replaced with a dead glare.

"You wanted this," she says. "You wanted me dead and gone. You wanted the fame for yourself."

With every word, her voice gets stronger, and her flesh a little more solid, as if with every word she is becoming more and more Rochelle.

"I didn't—" I say. "I swear I didn't ever want this to happen."

"Then why?" she wails. "Why didn't you fight for me? Why did you just leave me to get taken?"

"I tried!" I yell out. I glance back down to the phone between us. *This isn't Rochelle. This is just the game. Just the game!*

But her spiderlike hair forces me to look at her. Forces me to stare into her eyes. And as I do, I feel the ground beneath my feet give way. Feel the floor become a yawning abyss as the air turns to ice water.

I am floating.

No.

I am *sinking*.

"You did this to me, Beatrice," Rochelle's ghost growls. "You wanted me out of the way. You were always jealous of me, weren't you? Always wished you were as funny or as pretty. That's why you let the ghosts get me. You knew it was the only way you'd get the spotlight."

It's not true, I try to say, but the moment I open my lips, cold water rushes in. I seal them shut.

I want to struggle.

I know I should struggle to swim.

To reach the surface.

To escape.

But under Rochelle's glare, I can't move. I can't find the will to fight. All I can do is sink while her words drag me deeper.

"You know what the worst part is?" Rochelle asks. "The worst part is that you like Jacob more than me. My own brother, Beatrice! And you chose him over me. You could have saved me in the classroom, but you were too busy wanting to protect him."

186

I try to shake my head, but her hair binds me tight.
It's not true. It's not true.

But deep down, I fear it is.

Everything has been my fault.

No one would have been hurt if not for me.

The bathroom fades, becomes nothing but shadow and darkness, an endless abyss.

"Give up now," Rochelle says. "The game is over, Beatrice. You've lost. You always knew you'd lose, and because of you, you've lost everyone, too."

The weight of her words is an anchor. She is right.

"Give up," Rochelle whispers. "You're nothing without me. You're nothing at all. Give up, Beatrice. That's all you're good at. That's all you've ever done."

I sink. I feel the emptiness reach up to me.

I want to believe her words. Want to give up. To give in.

To lose.

But as I feel myself drown, a new sensation washes over me: determination.

No.

Rochelle—the ghost *pretending* to be Rochelle—is wrong.

I'm not a quitter. I've never given up.

And I'm not going to start now.

The moment I think it, the bathroom comes back

into focus. The water fades away, as if it never was.

I'm once more kneeling on the floor, stretching out for the phone on the bath mat.

The ghost woman—who no longer looks like Rochelle—hovers across from me.

Hair reaches to every corner of the bathroom, a giant spiderweb of deadly black strands.

Including a thick knot of hair that wraps around my neck, suffocating me.

The moment reality snaps back, there's a flash of recognition in the ghost's blank eyes—the knowledge I'm not giving in, the realization I'm fighting back. Her hair loosens, just a little, just for a split second.

I stretch forward—

grab the phone—

and in one quick movement, without even looking or trying to center, I raise the phone between us and take a picture.

Light flashes.

The ghost screams.

I flop back on the bathroom floor, released from her bonds, coughing and breathing as deeply as I can. The room swims, but not from any ghostly magic— from the sudden oxygen I hadn't known I was missing.

I look down at the screen.

DROWNED WOMAN CAPTURED

So that's what you were called, I think.
I open the glossary and click on her name.

> **A GHOST DROWNING NOT IN WATER,**
> **BUT IN MISERY.**
> **SHE WILL SHOW YOU YOUR DEEPEST**
> **FEARS, YOUR DARKEST REGRETS,**
> **UNTIL YOU JOIN HER IN THE DEPTHS**
> **OF HER DESPAIR.**

"Not today," I whisper.

When I can finally stand again, I blow-dry my hair and continue getting ready for bed.

I don't know why, but overcoming the Drowned Woman has filled me with resolve.

I'm not going to give up.

I'm going to fight.

37

I text Jacob a few hours later, telling him to watch the stream.

It's nearly eleven, and I'm back in the basement. All the lights are off save for the purple string lights behind the computer. The computer is running, cameras ready. Phone charged. My parents are sound asleep.

It's time.

I ready my phone, take a deep breath, and start the stream.

"Hey, everyone," I say. No cheesy intro this time. It's no longer a game. "It's just me tonight, Crimson. Well, actually, no. You should know my real name. Just in case. It's Beatrice. And my cohost . . ." The breath catches in my lungs. "My best friend, Butterfly? Her name is Rochelle. And she's . . . she's gone."

Already, there are a few dozen people logged into the feed, and the comments start pouring in.

Why are you giving your real names?
Is someone dead?
What's going on?
Is this an act?

"This isn't an act," I say. "This isn't for likes or views or subscriptions. This game is real. I didn't want to believe it at first and I know you won't either, but it's the truth. The ghosts are real, and so is the danger. They've already hurt a few people I know. That Tooth Fairy thing stole one of my dad's teeth. One of the Twins stole a classmate. And today . . ." Again, the catch of breath, the quick fight to keep myself from breaking into tears. "Today, Rochelle was taken. By one of the ghosts."

The feed instantly fills with comments of confusion and dismissal.

Yeah right.
Bet she's just sick.
This is such a stupid gimmick.

"I don't expect you to believe me," I say. "You weren't there. Though her brother was, so I'm not the only one who knows the truth. I just needed to tell you this, and film this, because . . . well, because I'm going to try to beat this game. It's the only way to get her back. But if I lose, I want it on camera. I want people to know what happened. So no one else falls prey to this game. And maybe, somehow, someone somewhere can hold the game's creators responsible."

I hold up my phone. But it's not the **DARK[room]** app. It's my camera roll.

"This is Rochelle," I say, showing the most recent picture of the two of us. One of the only remaining pictures of her I have. "She didn't deserve to be taken. She didn't deserve any of this. And this is what happened after she was taken." I swipe through the photos, the shots getting more and more blurry and faded, until I reach the photo of me with my arm around her ghost.

"These aren't manipulations," I say. "This is real. This game is dangerous, and it's dragged my friend to the Netherworld. And now, it's up to me to get her back."

The comments are blowing up. I don't read them.

"Now," I say, "let's play."

I close the photo app and go to open **DARK[room]**, but before I can, my phone buzzes.

A text.

I thought I had those silenced?

There's no preview, so I click the bubble and open the message.

Another message comes through.

This is a photo.

A picture of me in a desk chair, with purple string lights behind me. Staring down at my phone.

My skin prickles with dread.

I don't look up.

Another photo comes in.

And another.

And another.

They're all of me.

They're all of me right now. In this chair. Watching the texts come through.

Another text appears.

Another image.

Me, in the chair. And behind me, floating at both shoulders, the Twins.

I jerk and look up at the computer.

To see the Twins smiling at me, their sneering mouths wide.

"*Let's play, Beatrice.*" Their voices come in unison, from my phone and from the computer speakers.

The voices seem to come from everywhere. *"Hide-and-seek. If he finds you, you're dead!"*

My phone vibrates.

The clock switches to midnight—another ghost released.

And then, the computer and lights go dead.

38

Everything is blackness.

Everything except for the crackly white screen of my phone.

I quickly raise it up, scanning the basement, trying to track the giggling that most definitely isn't coming from any of the speakers. Faint flashes of white streak through the dark as the ghosts run and hide.

"Where are you?" I snarl.

More giggling.

"Show yourselves!" I demand, a little louder. I don't want to wake up my parents, but then again, maybe it's okay if they come down here. It's not that I think they can help, but at least then maybe I won't feel so alone. Maybe they'd start to believe me.

"Come find us!" the Twins call out in singsong unison. *"Come play!"*

I know it's a trap, but I don't have a choice. I flip on the phone's flashlight and follow the Twins through the dark.

The room my camera illuminates is not my basement.

Cobwebs drape like curtains from tall bare rafters, and the floor beneath my feet is dusty and rotted wood. I turn around, and the space my desk had been in is no longer there. All that exists are a few broken crates. I swear tiny eyes stare out through the cracks. I frantically cast the light around the room. Thick wooden beams support the crooked ceiling, and more than one jagged hole punctures the floor. All that's here are broken crates and spiderwebs and a darkness so thick, it coils in my lungs and makes it hard to breathe.

This is not my basement. This can't be real.

My legs freeze in place and my blood pounds in my ears.

Is this the Netherworld? Is this where they're keeping Rochelle?

Something rolls behind me.

I jump and turn around.

A tiny red ball rolls out from behind a crate and stops at my feet.

"*Play with us,*" the Twins call from the shadows.

"I'm not here to play these stupid games," I call out. "I'm here to beat you. I want my friend back."

Giggling.

Right

beside

my ear.

I jerk, but there's no one there.

"You have to play if you want her back," they say. Their unison voices dart around in the darkness, impossibly fast. *"Find us, and you find her."*

Anger burns in my chest as the Twins toy with me.

I swiftly raise the camera toward the last place I heard their voices and take a picture.

Light flashes, nearly blinding me.

But rather than a scream of defeat, the only thing that greets my attempt is another giggle.

I catch sight of pale white behind a crate and take another shot. I miss.

Another blur of movement on the other side of the room. I rush a few steps toward it and take a picture.

I miss again. Frustration grows inside me as I try to aim once more.

One Twin runs past me, shoving me to the side. I stumble and try to chase after it.

Two steps and my foot crashes through weak floorboards. I fall right through and drop hard to my knees. I don't drop my phone, thankfully. But when I look at it, I notice the screen is cracked.

The Twins cackle.

"*You'll have to try harder than that,*" one Twin says.

"*Maybe she needs inspiration,*" says the other.

"*I have an idea,*" they say as one.

Rochelle screams.

Her voice comes from everywhere and nowhere. I spin around, trying to find her, trying to get my stupid phone flashlight to illuminate something, *anything* that will tell me where she is. But the flashlight is flickering, and Rochelle is nowhere to be seen.

"Rochelle!" I yell out.

"Beatrice!" she yells back. "Help me!"

"Where are you?"

"*Nuh-uh-uhhh,*" the Twins say behind me.

I turn, and there they are, floating in the space before me. I jerk backward. Their blank eyes stare right through me. One holds the red ball in his tiny hand.

"*No cheating,*" they say. "*Unless you're a ghost. But if you're a ghost, that means we've won.*"

"Where is she?" I ask.

They smile.

"*The Moon Witch is coming for you,*" they say. "*She's almost here. Only a few more hours. And then she'll get you. Then you'll be dead.*"

I raise the camera and take a picture, but the Twins are too fast.

The moment the light flashes, they are beside me, one on each side.

"You'll have to play better than that if you want to beat her," one says.

    "You'll have to be faster. Much faster," says the other.

    "Especially if you want to outrun him."

One Twin tosses the ball behind me.

I turn and follow its roll with the flashlight.

The room transforms. Ceases being an abandoned warehouse.

The room

                        stretches

                                out.

It becomes a hallway lit with broken windows and scattered moonlight.

The hall from my nightmares.

The moment the ball stops, a new sensation races over my skin. A current of electricity. A cold dread.

A shadow moves at the far end of the hallway.

A shadow getting closer.

All I can see is the bulk of its torso, the hunched shoulders. Its arms stretch out to the sides, revealing skeletal fingers that extend to the wide walls like spider legs. Like razors.

The figure laughs, a deep, hungry belly chuckle.

I raise the camera. The flashlight flickers feebly, illuminating the figure like a strobe. In the cracked screen, the ghost looks even more terrifying.

I can see its moon-white eyes. Its jagged teeth and sharp smile.

Its name appears.

THE MAZE MASTER

I've found the next ghost.
Or . . . it has found me.

39

I don't wait for the Maze Master to come any closer.

I turn.

I need to run.

But there is nowhere to run *to*.

The strange warehouse I'd been trapped in is no more. Instead, I'm at a crossroads.

Hallways stretch to both sides and before me. They each look the same: rotted wooden floorboards, peeling white walls, cobweb-draped ceiling. Moonlit broken windows dot the halls, evenly spaced. Shadows conceal whatever awaits at their ends.

A high-pitched screeching noise wails behind me. I glance over my shoulder to see the Maze Master nearing; his nails scratch into the walls, peeling off spirals of paint. He's getting closer.

I run.

I don't even know which way I pick. Not that it matters—the moment I dart down the hall I'm met with another intersection, left or right. I dodge to the left, jumping over a pit in the floor and trying not to look back.

I can hear the Maze Master getting ever closer. And I know . . . no matter how fast I run, I'll never be able to escape him.

I turn another corner and nearly trip over the ghostly form of a Twin. He stands in the center of the hall, staring up at me with that wicked grin on his face.

"*Boo!*" he says with a laugh. Then he runs straight at me, knocking me over.

My phone goes flying.

The ghost child disappears behind me. The phone skids a dozen feet away.

Right at the feet of the Maze Master.

He laughs menacingly.

His shadowy face is hooked, his chin pointed out and down like a dagger or a crescent moon. His eyes are white pits, and in them, I see hallways. Endless hallways. I could get lost in that terrible stare for eternity. He reaches out toward me, his needle-like nails scratching the floors, the walls . . .

I force myself to look away, to scramble to my feet and take off again. I don't have a choice—I leave my phone, my only weapon, behind.

I race down the halls, leaping over creaking pits, dodging under broken rafters. My breath burns in my lungs and tears run down my face because no matter how fast I run, no matter how many turns I take, every time I look over my shoulder, he is there.

And he is getting closer.

"You'll never win, you know," the Twins say as I run by them. They sit on a crate along the wall, watching.

I don't answer. I round another corner, and they are there, standing in the middle of the hall.
"He's going to catch you," one says.

"And when he does . . ."

"Game over."

I ignore them, take a path to their right.

I can't tell if I've gone down this hallway before. I don't know if it even matters. I don't know if I have a chance of escaping.

I look behind me quickly.

No Twins.

No Maze Master. Maybe I'm safe. Maybe I've found an exit.

I look ahead.

And he is there.

Right in front of me.

I scream, try to change direction and run away. But when I turn, there is no hallway.

Just a wall.

Dead end.

I slam my fists against it.

It doesn't give.

The Maze Master doesn't talk. Just reaches out those spindly, jagged hands. He smiles wide.

I pound my fists harder against the wall and scream again.

"Let me out!" I yell. "Let me *out*!"

"Beatrice?!"

The light flips on as my mom's voice fills the hall.

No. Not the hallway.

The basement.

I'm back in the basement, pounding my hands against the wall like I've lost my mind, tears streaming down my face. I glance over and see that I'm only a few feet away from my computer desk. The camera is trained on me.

And I'm still streaming.

"What in the *world* is going on down here?" Mom asks, in her most no-nonsense tone. "Do you have any idea what time it is?"

I lower my fists.

I can't speak. I can barely even breathe.

What just happened?

What.

Just.

Happened?

"I—"

"Get up to your room," she says. "Now. And turn off all that computer stuff. We're going to have a long talk about this tomorrow. I've had enough with your games and streaming and lying. We're done!"

"I didn't—"

"Bed. Now!"

I go over to the computer. I try not to read the comments, though I can't help but skim a few. None of them are good.

is she for real?

why is she screaming?

what's going on?

So no one saw.

No one saw anything but me freaking out.

I don't even bother turning off the computer. I unplug it from the wall and plod back toward the stairs, toward my waiting mother, who stands there looking like she's ready to set me on fire or ground me for a millennium, whichever's worse.

I kick something on the ground along the way.

My phone.

I pick it up. The screen is cracked. So at least I wasn't hallucinating *everything*.

I don't hear anything Mom says when I walk past

her and into my room. I can't hear. Everything feels like it's underwater, myself included.

The game is taking over.

It's *taken* over.

And I'm losing.

I'm losing.

It's only when I'm in bed that I look at my phone again.

Through the cracked screen, I see about a dozen messages. All from Jacob. All asking if I'm okay. Because he was watching. He saw the whole thing. And yet, he saw nothing at all.

I don't respond.

I don't know how to.

I'm so exhausted, so numb, I don't even bother turning out the light.

I set my phone on the nightstand.

It buzzes right before I let it go.

Another text. Not from Jacob. From an unknown number.

That was fun.

Let's do it again.

THURSDAY

Final Day

40

The next morning, Jacob finds me on the way to school.

I barely even notice him falling into step beside me. I didn't sleep at all. My dreams were chaotic, filled with the Moon Witch chasing me down long hallways, the Twins laughing while the Maze Master spun a more horrible trap. Or I dreamed of Rochelle, screaming out for me, begging me to help her. And me failing, every single time.

"Bea?" he asks, and I realize that's not the first time he's tried to get my attention. "Are you in there?"

"What?" I ask.

He looks at me, his kind eyes concerned. "Are you okay? You're like the walking dead."

I try to shake the fog from my brain but don't quite succeed.

"I'm okay," I manage, right before a yawn escapes my lips. "I . . . I couldn't sleep."

"I couldn't either," he says. "Why didn't you text me back?"

A small stab of guilt spears through me. He'd texted at least another half-dozen times this morning, too. I didn't read any of them, let alone respond. What would I even say? *I'm sorry I'm the reason your sister is missing?*

"Sorry," I say.

"It's okay. I was just . . . I was worried about you. Last night. I mean. I don't even know what I saw. What happened?"

I glance around. Other kids are walking to school, and I notice more than one of them pausing to listen in.

"I don't want to talk about it," I say. *I don't want you to think I'm going out of my mind.*

"I get that," he says. "And I don't want to pressure you. But . . . Bea, we don't have much time. If we don't trap the other ghosts by midnight, it's game over."

We. We don't have much time.

Despite my bone-deep exhaustion, a little note of hope trills in my chest. Just at the thought that I might not be in this alone.

"I know, but . . ."

I look to the kids around us.

"Come on," he says. He takes my arm and pulls

me down an alley, away from our classmates. Away from our school.

"Where are we going?" I ask.

"My house," he replies. "My moms are at work."

"But we'll get in trouble for skipping," I say. Even as I say it, I know how stupid it sounds. What does it matter if we get in trouble for skipping? If I don't beat the game by midnight tonight, I won't be going back to school anyway.

He raises his eyebrow.

"Okay," I say. "Fine."

And maybe I should feel giggly or nervous about skipping school and going to Jacob's house when his parents are out. But all I feel is dread.

We're going to his place to play the game, and even though I know I have to, it's the last thing I want to do. About the only good feeling I have is the hope that maybe—together—we have a chance of beating this thing. Jacob is an avid gamer. If anyone can help me beat this game, it's him.

We head down the alley and make our way to his house, not even trying to stay hidden. We've already missed the first bell by ten minutes, and I keep waiting for someone to jump out from a doorway and scold us for playing hooky, or for a cop to drive by and drag us back to school. But none of that happens. No one looks at us twice as we walk down the sidewalk. No one calls out to stop us as we make our way up his front steps. No one demands to know why we're not in school and instead going into a house where there are no parents.

It's ridiculously easy. Which almost makes me more nervous.

"Okay," he says when we're inside. He leads me into the dining room, and we sit across from each other at the table. It feels so familiar. We've sat at these seats dozens of times in the past. But in all those instances, Rochelle was here, sitting in the chair to my left. It feels strange being here without her.

It makes her absence more apparent.

"Okay?" I reply.

"Tell me everything that happened last night," he says.

"What did you see?" I ask him.

He bites his lip and looks away.

"It was . . . strange," he says. "I saw you start the game. Saw the Twins racing around the room and tormenting you. Then the screen went grainy and glitched out for a second, and when it came back you were standing by the wall and slamming your fists and screaming."

"But, wait," I say. "What do you mean, a second later? I was trapped in there for at least half an hour."

"Trapped where?" he asks. "What did you see?"

My mind churns. Not only had the game glitched out my computer and messed up my feed, but it had somehow manipulated time. I know I was trapped in that maze for longer than a second or two.

What did the Maze Master do to me?

I pull out my phone and place it on the table between us, so he can see the screen. As always, it's open to the **DARK[room]** app already.

"What are you doing?" he asks.

"I need to check something." I'd been so exhausted, so completely drained last night, I hadn't even considered checking the ghost glossary.

I pull it up and open the Maze Master's profile.

THE MAZE MASTER RULES THE NETHERWORLD.
TIME AND SPACE ARE HIS TO MANIPULATE.
ONCE HE HAS YOU IN HIS MAZE,
YOUR ONLY ESCAPE
IS HIS DEFEAT.
OR YOURS.

My heart thuds in my chest.

If my mom hadn't turned on the light when she did . . .

"You found the next ghost," Jacob whispers.

I look at him. Despite everything, I still feel butterflies when our eyes meet.

"Yeah," I say. "And he nearly got me."

Then I take a deep breath and tell him everything that had happened.

41

I stand in the doorway to Rochelle's bedroom.

Jacob is downstairs, making a quick snack since neither of us was able to eat this morning.

It feels strange being in here without her. Wrong.

We'd spent so many hours in here. Every inch of this space is a memory.

Hiding from the summer heat in the air-conditioning, playing co-op games on our laptops on her bed.

Sitting on the giant beanbag in the corner, reading our way through her extensive manga collection.

Setting up a secondhand sewing machine on her desk so we could sew our own cosplay costumes. And then a few extra things, like a skirt and velvet corset and a full jester outfit, because we were convinced we would make it to a Renaissance Faire, even though the nearest was a three-hour drive away.

I walk over to her dresser and pick up one of the photos. Her and me on Halloween, dressed as our favorite *Sailor Moon* characters. (I was Mercury, she was Jupiter. We'd even managed to convince Jacob to dress up as Tuxedo Mask in one of my dad's old, poorly fitting suits. He refused to be in the photo, though.) We're on the front porch, smiling, surrounded by Halloween decorations—pumpkins glowing on the railings, fabric ghosts billowing from the trees. I'm honestly relieved to find a picture with her in it. She's now been erased from all the pictures on my phone.

Wait.

I squint and bring the photo closer.

One of the fabric ghosts isn't fabric at all.

The image blurs as I stare at it.

The ghost shifts. Billows.

Becomes a woman in a white dress, bound in red ropes.

The Moon Witch.

I watch in horror as she places a hand on Rochelle's shoulder.

Rochelle's eyes widen in fear, her mouth opening in a silent scream.

Her image begins to fade.

"No," I whisper. "No, you can't!"

The Moon Witch smiles wider as she drags Rochelle away.

"*You are too late,*" the Moon Witch coos in my mind. "*She is mine now, and you will never get her back.*"

Rochelle is on the brink of vanishing entirely. I shake the photo.

"No. Rochelle!"

"Hey," Jacob says behind me. "Are you okay?"

I look over to see him standing in the doorway. He has a bag of chips and a plate stacked with peanut butter and jelly sandwiches in his hands.

"It—I—she—"

I hold up the photo.

"What?" he asks. He inspects it. "What's wrong?"

I flip the photo back around. In the image, Rochelle is there beside me, smiling like before. The Moon Witch is nowhere to be seen.

"She was gone," I whisper. "The Moon Witch had taken her. Just like all the photos on my phone."

I'd shown him those, too, when telling him about what happened last night.

He doesn't tell me I'm losing it. He hasn't this entire time. I set the photo back down on the dresser.

"We'll get her back," he says. He holds out the sandwiches. "Here, take one. We'll need our energy if we're going to beat this thing."

I take the sandwich and follow him out of Rochelle's room. I look over my shoulder at the photos.

Rochelle is missing.

From every

    single

    one.

42

"I'm surprised it hasn't gone off at all today," I say, staring at my phone.

The cell phone charges on Jacob's computer desk. It doesn't buzz. Doesn't blink.

The only messages I've gotten so far are from my mom, demanding to know where I am and why she got a call from the school saying I wasn't there.

I don't respond. Obviously. I have bigger things to worry about.

Jacob briefly glances from his computer to the phone, then back again. We're logging into all of my streaming accounts and synching our devices so we can stream. If this is going to be the last battle, we need to get it on camera. Just so people know what happened.

Just so this doesn't happen to anyone else, ever again.

"Maybe the game is scared," Jacob suggests.

I laugh, and he raises an eyebrow.

"What?" he asks. "Seriously: It's the final day. You

just have to capture a few more ghosts and then you win. So maybe it's just hiding until midnight, trying to cheat so you don't have a chance at winning."

A part of me wants to say it can't be that smart, but I know the game is.

"Then it's not going to like what we're about to do," I say.

The plan is simple. It's the same plan I've had before, except this time I have someone to help: We're going to play until we win. We have a couple spare battery packs. A pile of snacks. Multiple cameras set up around the room, plus a portable. And, most importantly, an entire house to ourselves for the rest of the day, so no one else can get hurt.

So long as we win before his moms get home.

I glance over to him. My heart flips when I look at his face, at his dark curls and furrowed, concentrating brow. He's not the little kid who used to play dolls with me and Rochelle. He looks older. Not just because he *is* older, but because this whole experience has already aged him.

"We're going to find her," I say, steeling my voice with resolve. "I know Rochelle is still in there. In the Netherworld. We're going to get her back."

He looks over at me, a small smile on his face, and I swear I see relief flash over his features, just for an instant. As if my saying it could make it true, could make him believe it.

"I know," he says. "I have faith in you."

The warmth in my chest grows.

It's hard to explain it, but I believe him. With Rochelle, yeah, she had faith in me. But only to a degree. I mean, she's my best friend. But she isn't the type to just trust someone. You have to earn that trust. And she is a skeptic, which is why she didn't fully believe me about the ghosts in the first place. Jacob, however, hasn't doubted or questioned me for a moment. Even now, with his sister missing, he seems to trust me completely.

I don't know if anyone has done that before. Not even my parents.

I realize then that I'm just staring at him, so I clear my throat and look away. Now is not the time to be crushing.

"Okay, then," I say. "Let's do this."

He nods.

I grab my phone, and he starts the stream.

"Hey, everyone," I say into the camera. "I'm here with Rochelle's brother, Jacob. It's our last day to beat this game before the Moon Witch appears, and after last night, well . . . After last night it's pretty apparent that I need to beat this as fast as I can." I pause, looking from the camera to Jacob, and then back again. "I know a lot of you are wondering what happened last night. I wish I could have shown you. Maybe then you'd believe me. Maybe then you'd know to leave the game alone. Because last night, I was dragged into the Netherworld. I know you couldn't see it. You just have to believe me. And that's why I'm filming again now. Because today . . ." I swallow. "Today I'm not going to stop playing the game until I've beaten it and gotten Rochelle back. Or until it kills me. And I want the world to know what happened."

I flip my phone around to show the camera.

"I've downloaded an app that is going to record everything that appears on my phone screen. So even if the external cameras don't pick anything up, you'll still get to see what I see in the app. Even if one or both of us don't make it, the world will still get to see what happened. What *really* happened."

I swallow. The weight of this is really starting to hit home.

There's a chance we won't make it out of this alive.

There's a chance we'll fail.

"And Mom, Dad . . . I'm sorry," I say. "I just . . . yeah."

I look away and sniff back tears, pretending to fidget with my phone.

"Okay," I say. "I'm ready. Let's start the game."

Jacob stands away from the computer and comes up beside me, holding a camcorder.

I turn on my forehead camera.

I open the **DARK[room]** app.

The screen crackles.

It's strange looking around someone else's room in the app, strange seeing his bed and bookshelves and gaming console turned into a grayscale nightmare. Maybe it's because sun is streaming in. Maybe it's because a basement has its own creep factor. But as I look at the camera, it hits me just how not-scary this looks. Especially to an outsider. I mean, it's just a grainy screen and an occasional jump scare. It's not nearly so frightening when the ghosts aren't haunting *you*.

For the briefest moment, it's easy to see this as an outsider, to think it's all just some big trick or scam. It's easy to think it's just a game.

Then my phone vibrates. And when it does, the light above us flickers.

"Did you see that?" I ask.

"Yeah," Jacob replies. "Maybe it isn't hiding after all."

"No," I whisper. "Because it knows it's going to win."

I scan the room. I don't expect anything to be in here, but the vibrations get stronger.

Especially when I center the phone on his closet door.

"I think there's something in there," I whisper.

My phone pulses stronger as I take a hesitant step forward.

"Wait," he whispers. "I think—"

I hear it then. A long, slow

creeeeeeeeeeeeeak.

And it's not coming from the phone.

The closet door is opening.

"Are you seeing this?" I whisper.

"Yeah," he replies in a nervous hush.

The closet door stops.

Nothing happens.

Nothing moves.

I don't even think that I breathe.

And then, a small red ball rolls from the closet, stopping right at Jacob's foot.

"Okay," I say when the ball stops. "Are you seeing *that*?"

He bends down slowly and picks up the ball, examining it.

"Yeah," he breathes. He looks to the camera. "And for the record, we are completely alone."

I take the ball from him.

"It's the same one from last night," I say. "The Twins were playing with it in the Netherworld. How did it get here?"

Giggling comes from the closet.

"I think we're about to find out," Jacob says. He steps forward and—before I can tell him to be careful—opens the closet door.

It isn't a closet staring back.

Instead, a long, shadowy hallway stretches in front of us. Everything is a muted gray, from the cobweb-draped rafters to the dilapidated wooden floors and peeling white walls.

Jacob lets out a long breath, almost a whistle.

"Is that . . . ?" he asks.

"The Netherworld," I reply with a nod. I look at my phone—the screen mirrors the hall in front of us. No ghosts to be seen, but I know they're near.

I also know that—even if the other cameras aren't getting this—the screen is recording. The world is seeing what we're seeing. *You aren't getting away that easily,* I think.

"Come on," I say. "Let's get some ghosts."

I step past Jacob, into the hallway. The moment I'm in, the air drops twenty degrees and a dusty, musty smell clogs my lungs. My feet echo and creak on the wooden planks. Jacob follows close behind me, expertly keeping the camera trained on me and my phone.

"I don't know if the cameras are catching this," I say, "but we're stepping into the Netherworld now. It's the same hallway I was in last night. Which means the Maze Master isn't far off."

We walk a few more feet, peering into shadows, waiting for a ghost to appear as my phone constantly pulses and Jacob breathes heavily beside me.

SLAM!

I leap and turn at the noise behind us. The closet door is now shut, and as I watch, the brown wood bleaches to gray spiderwebs with dust and cracks. Jacob races forward and grabs the rusted black handle. I don't expect it to open, but he yanks it easily.

His room isn't behind the door, not like it should be. Instead, it's just the endless hallway.

"We're trapped," he says. He looks to me, eyes wide, and I realize that he's just now truly afraid. Just now truly understanding how real and how dangerous this actually is.

And this is only the beginning.

43

We wander slowly down the hall, swinging our cameras all around us in hopes we find something. But the phone doesn't vibrate, the cameras don't pick up any disturbances. The only sound is our creaking footsteps, the occasional hush of wind. Our breath comes out in clouds that glitter in the shafts of moonlight. Neither of us says a thing.

Soon, the hallway branches off. We pause in the crossroads, inspecting each hall with our cameras, hoping to find something—some clue, some hint of where Rochelle or the ghosts might be.

Silence.

I think of what Jacob said, about how the ghosts might just be hiding, biding their time until midnight when it's game over. At this rate, the ghosts won't even *have* to attack us. The Maze Master could just keep conjuring these endless hallways, trapping us until we run out of time. Finding Rochelle will be the least of our worries if we manage to trap ourselves here.

The only way out is to capture the ghosts. How can we capture them if they don't appear?

After a few more minutes of wandering aimlessly, after a few more hallways that only lead to more hallways, I stop in the middle of an intersection.

"We're getting nowhere like this," I say in frustration. I look back down the hallway we just came from. Or was it the one to my left? I can't keep track anymore. "We need to draw out the ghosts, or we'll never find Rochelle."

Jacob bites his lip and thinks for a bit.

"Well," he says finally, "the Twins like games, right? So maybe we play a game to draw their attention."

"Like what?"

He shrugs. "I don't know . . . hide-and-seek?"

My jaw drops. "You can't be serious. You want to split up? That's, like, the one thing you're never supposed to do."

"Do you have any other ideas?"

"Anything other than splitting up." I take a deep breath. "Wait. What about tag? That way we're not splitting up, not really."

He considers. "That might work."

"Better than nothing," I say. "Come on, let's try." I slap him on the shoulder. "Tag, you're it!"

"Hey!" he yelps.

I take off.

Jacob is close on my heels. I don't run too fast—I don't actually want to lose him, but I want it to be convincing.

As I dart down another hall, I hear giggling. My heart leaps with hope.

I don't see the Twins, but I can hear them. Just as I hear Jacob's feet thudding behind me, I hear their tiny footsteps pattering on the floorboards around and in front of me.

Keeping up. Keeping chase.

Someone smacks me on the arm and I let out a scream.

"You're it!" Jacob yells.

He skids to a stop and then runs away from me.

"I thought you were a ghost!" I call out.

"Not yet!" he responds.

He runs, and I realize then that he is much, much faster than me. And he isn't restraining himself like I was. He races down the hall and I push myself to keep up. He's far enough ahead that the darkness is starting to swallow him up. He looks like a shadow.

He looks like a ghost.

"Slow down!" I yell. We're just supposed to attract the Twins, not actually try to escape from each other.

But he must not hear me because he doesn't slow down. Breath burns in my lungs as I push myself to catch up to him.

He rounds a corner.

"Wait!" I yell.

Someone giggles in the darkness beside me. I don't look over.

"*This is fun*," says one of the Twins. "*But we prefer your first suggestion. Let's play hide-and-seek. We hide your friends, and you seek them before it's too late.*"

I round the corner.

It's a dead end.

And Jacob is nowhere to be seen.

44

"Jacob!" I yell. I run over and slam my fists against the wall. The wood cracks, but it doesn't give.

I scream out in frustration.

"Where are you?!" I yell out. "What have you done with him?"

"You wanted to play games, didn't you?" a Twin asks behind me.

I turn around, but he darts off before I catch sight of him.

"Well," says the other, *"we wanted to play too."*

I turn to face him, but he vanishes into the shadows.

"No more games!" I yell.

"But we're having so much fun," says one of the Twins. *"We could play like this forever."*

"Until the Moon Witch shows up," says the other.

I keep looking around, trying to find them, but they dart away into the shadows, impossibly fast.

"Then she will take you away."

"Far, far away. So we must have as much fun as we can before then."

"Where did you take Jacob?" I demand.

"Sent him away. Hide-and-seek!"

Frustration builds inside me. But so does a note of hope: I wanted them to show themselves. And even though Jacob isn't here to help, I still have a job to do. I just have to hope I can pull it off.

I turn on the spot and take a picture without even looking to see if I'm close.

Light flashes, and childish giggling follows. In that brief blast, I see the faces of the Twins in the darkness, right before they dart off into the shadows. I take another photo before my vision even clears.

"You'll never get us like that," they say in unison.

"Never ever ever!"

I track their voices and take another photo.

"Hey! That was close!"

Another flash, another missed shot.

Something small barrels into my leg, knocking me to the ground.

"If you won't play fair, we'll take it away!"

Tiny hands latch onto my arms, and another set grabs for my phone, begins tugging it away. I can barely see in the darkness. I struggle against them as they wrestle the phone from my hands.

"No!" I yell out. I can't lose it. It's my only weapon.

"Give! It! Here!"

I yell out as they manage to yank the phone from my hand.

"Come and get it!" they say, cackling.

They run.

I scramble to my feet and chase after them.

They dart down hallways, ducking in and out shadows, tossing my phone back and forth between them. I'd have lost them if not for the constant glow of my screen. For the first time, I'm actually grateful that the **DARK[room]** app stays open.

They run for what feels like ages, though the endless unchanging hallways make it hard to tell how far we've actually gone.

"Give me back my phone!" I yell out.

They only giggle in response.

But then, as they near another intersection of hallways, something bursts from the side hall, slamming through one of the Twins.

"Jacob!" I yell.

"Quick!" he calls back in response, tossing something toward me.

My phone! He'd tackled into the Twins and stolen back my phone!

"No!" one of the Twins screams out. *"How could you! Cheater!"*

The Twin flings himself at Jacob, tiny fists punching. Jacob vainly tries to defend himself.

I take the opportunity.

I raise the phone.

I center the screen.

And when it pulses, I take the shot.

Light flashes.

The Twin screams out.

And when the flash fades, it's just Jacob standing in the center of the hall, his arms still raised to defend himself from a ghost that is no longer there.

"Is that it?" he asks. "Did we get them?"

We stand there in silence for a long while. I scan the phone around the hallway, but nothing vibrates. Perhaps, in catching one of them, I captured both.

"I think so," I say.

Jacob smiles wide and runs over to me, wrapping me in a hug.

"You did it," he says.

And even though we're trapped in some twisted Netherworld maze, his hug makes me feel warm. Safe. Just for a moment, I can pretend everything is okay. Just for a moment, before he steps back.

"I thought I lost you," he says.

"Me too," I reply. "What happened?"

He shrugs. "I don't really know."

"Why did you run so fast?" I ask.

"I didn't think I was?" he replies, questioningly. "I kept looking back and you were always right behind me. Until I looked back, and it was just a dead end. I kept running around, trying to find you. When I heard you calling out, I managed to track you down."

"The Maze Master is playing tricks on us," I mutter.

"Well, it's our turn to play tricks of our own," he replies. "You caught the Twins. Now we just need to capture him."

"But how? He's probably hiding."

Jacob's smile comes back.

"I was thinking about that," he says. "And I have an idea."

45

"They always keep the treasure at the center of a maze, right?" Jacob asks. "Like, in all the myths and stuff. That's the safest place. And that's also where they keep their biggest guards. So if Rochelle is anywhere, she's there. So is the Maze Master."

"But that still doesn't solve how we find her," I say.

"Maybe we can call her," he says. "You know her—she always keeps her phone fully charged. There's a chance we'll be able to hear it ring and follow it back to her. Just like you calling out helped lead me to you."

"That's a brilliant idea," I say.

"I thought so," he replies with a dashing wink. "I'll call her phone so you can keep the app running. If we run into any more ghosts, don't think—take the picture. We can't let anything get in our way. Something just doesn't feel right about all this. Like . . . I don't know—I know we just got here, but it feels like hours have gone past. Or maybe it's just me."

I don't say anything to that, because I know exactly how he feels. I'm exhausted. Like I've been running all day. But it's only been a few minutes. An hour, tops. Right?

I push the fear down and ready my phone.

He reaches into his pocket, pulls out his own phone, and dials her number.

A few seconds stretch by. I wonder if phones will even work here, if her phone is charged, or if she even has it still.

And then I hear it.

Far down the hall, faint as a wind chime. Rochelle's ringtone.

"It's her," I whisper.

Jacob breaks into a smile, and I feel myself grinning as hope blooms in my chest. For the first time, it actually feels like we might have a chance.

"Keep calling her," I say.

He nods.

He keeps his camera rolling. He keeps calling Rochelle's phone.

We make our way down the hall, following the ringtone that gets louder and louder with every successful junction. I keep my phone out, keep scanning the hall before and behind us. But it doesn't vibrate. No ghosts appear.

The ringtone gets louder.

We have to be getting close.

"I don't like this," I whisper. I keep my eyes on my phone. I keep waiting for something to appear, for some hint of a ghost. Nothing.

"What? We're nearly there. You're the one who said we should find her first."

"I know, it just . . . this feels too easy."

He shrugs. "You have to keep thinking of it like a video game. Sometimes there's a glitch or cheat." He holds up his phone, still dialing Rochelle's number. "I think we found it."

I nod, but I don't feel any better.

We come to another crossroads and follow the ringtone to the right. We head to the very end, to where the hall changes course and goes left. The ringing stops. We follow the hallway around anyway.

Into not another hallway, but a room.

It looks like a warehouse, like the room I stumbled into the first time I was taken to the Netherworld. Splintered wooden crates pile against cracked pillars. Cobwebs billow from the rafters. Shadows twist and seethe above and around us, with only the moonlight from a dozen broken windows illuminating the space.

That light is enough.

Enough to make out a shape suspended in the center of the room. A shape wrapped tight in a thousand black threads. Cocooned. Her hair hanging over her limp face.

Rochelle.

46

"Rochelle!" Jacob calls out. We race toward her, though once we reach her we realize just how bad this situation is.

Rochelle looks even worse up close. Her eyes are heavily lidded and sweat drips from her forehead even though it's cold as ice in here. She doesn't move when we approach. She doesn't even flinch when Jacob grabs for the thin black strands that envelop her.

But he does.

"Ouch!" he hisses. He draws back his hands and stares at his palms in horror.

Thin red lines are already burned into his skin.

"What in the world?" he whispers.

I reach out and gingerly touch one of the threads. Instantly, a shock of pain lances through my body, electric and acidic and burning like fire.

My finger blisters red.

"Isn't yours to take, she's not," hisses a voice behind us. I turn, ice pooling in my heart, and see the Maze Master towering in a doorway.

His hooked face glowers at us, his long-taloned fingers grazing the floor. And I see, now, that spiderwebs of darkness spiral out from those fingertips wherever they touch. Like fissures in reality. Like webs of illusion.

"She isn't yours to keep!" I yell out.

I raise my camera and take a photo.

Light flashes, and in the screen I catch a glimpse of the Maze Master raising his hand, black threads spreading in the air before him.

When the light clears, he is gone. But he hasn't been captured.

"Not so easy," he growls. *"My maze. My home. Not yours. I hunt, not you!"*

I flinch back as something whips past my face.

Black threads.

They snap toward the floor. And where they touch, the wood changes. Bubbles. Burns away. Becomes a hole. A hallway in the floor, leading to darkness.

I raise my camera and take a shot where I think the threads came from, but I know before I even click the button that I missed.

Another thread shoots past me, coming from the

opposite direction. If not for Jacob's quick shove, it would have hit me.

Around us, the room begins to change.

Rochelle's limp body is lifted high above us while the floor and the walls shudder and shift. Walls rise from the floorboards, hallways melt from the walls. A wall rises between Rochelle and us, blocking her from view. The room reshapes itself, becomes twisted white hallways that stretch in every direction—up and down and left and right.

"What's happening?" I ask. I cower against Jacob, trying not to stumble as vertigo hits and the room twists and twines impossibly.

"He's fighting back," Jacob says beside me. "Making it so we can't get to him. Or Rochelle." He looks around. "Come on," he says.

We head down a hall—one that isn't defying the laws of physics—but quickly hit a dead end. When we turn around to backtrack, the hall shifts, rotates straight up. Jacob groans in frustration while the Maze Master laughs.

"We're never going to get anywhere like this," Jacob says. "He can control everything here. He'll never let us get close to her. Or to him." His expression changes, just for a second, a strange mix of hopeful and scared. "Unless . . ."

"Unless what?" I ask.

He shakes his head. "Just be ready, okay?" he whispers.

"I . . ."

He puts a finger to his lips. Then he looks up at the ceiling, which is actually just another floor. My stomach twists. Are *we* on the ceiling?

Jacob walks away from me.

"I want my sister back, you creep!"

"*Not yours,*" the Maze Master replies from everywhere and nowhere at once. "*Mine.*"

"Then we trade," Jacob says. "You take me, and you give her back."

I can practically feel the Maze Master smiling.

Threads drape down in front of us, unfurling like thin black fern fronds, creating a tapestry of darkness. The Maze Master appears within them, peeling out from the curtain, his hooked face smiling.

"*Why trade?*" he says. "*You're all mine. All mine to keep. Foolish, stupid children! Trapped forever. Mine!*"

He reaches out a taloned hand and lances of black shoot from his long fingertips, wrapping whip fast around Jacob.

Jacob yells out. But he doesn't try to run away or break free. I feel frozen in terror as I watch the Maze

Master hover closer to him, towering over Jacob, a cat cornering its prey.

And that's when I realize what Jacob meant by *be ready.*

While the Maze Master is distracted with ensnaring Jacob, I raise my camera. I center it on the Maze Master's face.

The camera vibrates, the screen glows.

At the last second, the Maze Master looks at me. His face is pure fury. My screen cracks.

I take the shot.

My camera vibrates so intensely that I drop it. It falls from my fingers and

> ever
>
> so
>
> slowly
>
> tumbles
>
> > to
> >
> > > the
> > >
> > > > floor.

The Maze Master disintegrates in a billow of black threads, and as he disappears, the walls around us break down, bursting outward so slowly it feels like a dream. The threads around Jacob unravel.

I take a step forward, or try to—my legs feel like they're dragging through wet concrete.

There's a *whoosh*, a rush of air.

When my raised foot finally lands, it doesn't land on the broken wood floor of the Netherworld.

It lands on carpet.

I blink and look around.

We're in Jacob's bedroom.

47

Jacob stands before me. Rochelle is draped on the bed, out cold. My phone is on the carpet behind me, and Jacob's computer and streaming setup still runs in the corner.

We stand there for a split second, staring at each other, trying to get our brains to catch up to reality. Then, as one, we rush over to Rochelle's side.

"Is she okay?" I ask.

He sets down his camcorder and pats her on the side of the face, hovers the back of his hand over her lips.

Her eyelids flutter.

"Yeah," he whispers. "She's breathing. Just out cold."

I gasp and nearly cry in relief as tears fill my eyes. I lean against Jacob, who just wraps an arm around me, as though it's the most natural thing in the world.

It *feels* like the most natural thing in the world.

"We did it," I whisper. "We beat the game. It's over."

We crouch there for a while, staring at his sister.

Relief floods through me, slowly washing away the panic. Rochelle looks so beautiful, bathed in the moonlight—I don't think I've ever been so relieved to see her before.

Wait. *Moonlight?*

I look to the window. Sure enough, it's completely dark outside, only the light of the full moon illuminating the room. But we started streaming this morning—how is it so late?

"Jacob?" I ask as he pets Rochelle's hair. "Jacob, what time is it?"

He looks to the window, where I'm staring, and then looks to a clock on the opposite wall.

"Ten minutes to midnight," he says. It sounds like a gasp. "How is that possible?"

"I don't know," I say. I grab my phone off the carpet. The **DARK**[room] app is still running. The hairs on the back of my neck rise.

"Well," Jacob says, "at least we beat the game before time was up. Ten minutes to spare!" He checks the clock again. "Well, nine."

"Something isn't right," I whisper. "Why is the game still running?"

"I don't know," Jacob replies. "But we did it, we got Rochelle back."

Then I think . . .

The Devouring Woman, The Tooth Fairy, The Twins, The Drowned Woman, The Broken Man, The Maze Master . . .

"Six," I say.

"What?"

"Six ghosts. We captured six ghosts."

"I—"

"There's still one more."

I hold up the phone to double-check the glossary while Jacob goes on about how maybe we beat it anyway, because the final ghost hasn't appeared and it's almost midnight.

And as I raise the phone, Rochelle comes into screen.

The moment she does, my phone starts to vibrate.

48

"J-Jacob," I stammer. "Jacob get back!"

Three words have appeared on my buzzing phone.

THE MOON WITCH

Jacob looks at me for a moment, confused. But then Rochelle starts to laugh. It isn't her voice.

It's the voice of the ghost I'd seen in my dreams. The Moon Witch.

Jacob starts to stand, but before he can move, red ropes lash out from underneath his bed, wrapping around his ankles and arms, twisting around him, and raising him up into the air. He floats like a marionette in the middle of his room, while on the bed, the Moon Witch rises.

Her laugh is a vicious cackle, one that fills the room with malice and cold dread.

She floats up, and in the moonlight she looks like Rochelle.

But the moment she floats forward, out of the shaft of moonlight, she transforms.

Rochelle's beautiful dark skin turns pale and crisps away, strips drifting down to the floor like paper to reveal a skeletal face with bloodshot eyes. Her clothes blur to white, becoming a tattered dress that is more cobweb than fabric. Her braids unravel into a halo of twisting strands, and red ropes twine around her torso. She raises her gnarled hands, and Jacob floats over to the wall, where ghostly hands peel out of the wallpaper and grab him tight. He yells out, but a hand clamps over his mouth.

But the Moon Witch isn't watching him.

She is staring straight at me, her skull cracked in a smile.

"*You thought it would be so easy, Beatrice?*" she asks. Her voice is velvet, even now, and somehow more terrifying coming from her skinless skull. "*You may have captured my minions, but you should have known that no game can be won that easily. Especially now that I have the energy of your friends running through my bones.*"

"What have you done with her?" I demand. My voice cracks, but I'm surprised by my own resolve. *Them?* I wonder. Then I remember—she trapped Claire, too.

"*Nothing,*" she says. "*Yet.*"

She cackles, and I remember that this is still a game. There is still a timer. And according to the clock on the wall, I only have a few minutes left.

I still have a job to do.

I raise the phone and take a picture.

Light flashes, but the Moon Witch doesn't scream in rage. Even though I know I centered the frame on her. Even though I know it should have worked.

"*Silly child,*" she says when the light clears. She still floats in front of me. "*Did you think that would be enough? Your silly toy cannot harm me. It is too weak. But since you want to play, let us play.*"

She smiles, and I wonder momentarily what she means.

The next moment, she floats backward into the moonlight. Her shape changes, once more becomes the beautiful woman I'd seen in my dreams. But she doesn't stop changing. The air around her blurs, and I watch in horror as her image stretches out to the sides.

Multiplies.

The shapes blur and replicate, and soon the room is filled with her terrifyingly beautiful likeness.

They float around me, swapping places, until I have no idea which is the real Moon Witch and which are the duplicates. What's more, hundreds of red ropes stretch to every corner of the room, obscuring Jacob, obscuring our streaming setup. All I can clearly see is the clock on the wall, counting down the seconds until I have failed everyone.

The ghosts flicker between the ropes, unimpeded.

And then they start to attack.

49

Ghosts pummel into me from all sides.

I yelp in pain as a Moon Witch scratches at my face. I take a picture, and she disappears in a flash of light, but the other replicas continue their attack.

I stumble backward and trip over a rope as another ghost comes for me.

I scream out. But I realize I'm not the only one crying in pain.

I look over to see Rochelle—the *real* Rochelle— bound in red rope farther away. Rope is wrapped around her eyes, but she cries out in pain. Another cry rips out from the other direction, and through the tangle of ropes I see Claire. They both yell out, and I know then that the ropes are squeezing them. That soon, if I don't act, they will die.

I scramble toward Rochelle, climbing through the ropes that stretch and trip, taking photos of the imposter ghosts that swoop and claw. Every time I capture one, another swoops back to take its place.

"Rochelle!" I scream out. "Rochelle, I'll save you!"

Another ghost swoops toward me. I take a shot, and she disappears—but not before knocking the phone from my hands. The phone falls to the ground behind me, away from Rochelle. I turn to grab it.

When I turn back around, Rochelle is nowhere to be seen.

"Rochelle!" I cry.

Her scream answers, this time coming from the opposite direction.

Around me, the Moon Witch cackles.

"Isn't this what you wanted?" the Moon Witch calls out as one of her terrifying replicas swoops at me. I take a picture, and the ghost disappears without a sound as the real Moon Witch carries on. *"You wanted to be the center of attention, Beatrice. You wanted everyone to watch. And now they are. You have thousands of eyes trained on you, Beatrice. Watching you fail. Watching you lose. Watching you be the reason your friends will die."*

Another ghost swoops toward me. I take a picture.

And an idea forms as the replica vanishes.

Thousands of people watching.

I scramble back to my feet, camera raised and taking photos at everything that moves. Rochelle screams, as does Claire, and from another direction I hear Jacob yelling in pain, too.

"*Hear their cries, Beatrice?*" the Moon Witch calls. "*Hear how they need you? Hear how you are failing them, even now? Find them, before it is too late!*"

But I don't climb between ropes in search of my friends. I head instead to the computer in the corner—I can just make it out through the maze of red ropes.

I know what the Moon Witch is doing.

She is trying to distract me. Trying to run out the clock.

And she is winning.

I reach the computer.

On the monitor, I see my terrified face, blood dripping from scratches in my cheek and a bruise forming over my eye. I can see the viewer count, can see the comments rolling in, the thousands of viewers wondering if this is still a prank, or if this is real.

I can see the clock.

I only have a minute left.

I stare straight into the camera.

"I know you think this is a joke. A game. It's not. It's real. And I need your help. When I say *now*, take a screenshot. Please!"

I don't know if this will work, but it's the only shot I have left. Literally.

I raise my phone, make sure that the screen is visible in the computer camera. In the computer monitor, I see the app screen. Thousands of people around the world are watching through this lens, seeing this scene. The tangle of red ropes, the single form of the Moon Witch, darting between them.

"I give up!" I yell out. Only seconds left. "Please! Just give me my friends back. Take me instead!"

The Moon Witch appears in front of me. And I know it is the real one—my phone buzzes wildly as it centers on her, as her name appears in the bottom of the screen.

"*You will be mine for eternity*," she says. "*All of you!*" She points straight to me.

Straight to the computer screen.

"Now!" I yell.

I take the picture.

As I do, thousands of viewers take a photo as well, their screenshots amplifying the power of my camera, photographing her face on thousands of screens across the world.

Blinding light flashes. The Moon Witch screams.

My phone cracks in half.

And as the light clears, as the pieces of my phone clatter to the floor, I blink away the brightness.

No more ropes.

No more Moon Witch.

Just Jacob standing against the far wall. And pounding coming from the closet.

I race forward and yank open the door, and Rochelle tumbles out. Rochelle falls into my arms, sobbing, asking to know what happened. Jacob comes over and puts a hand on my shoulder.

"It's a long story," he says. "And you won't believe it, but we caught it all on camera."

Epilogue

"You're sure you want to do this?" Rochelle asks. "I mean, after everything we've accomplished . . ."

"I know," I say. "I know."

We are in my basement. Jacob is lounging on the sofa while she and I sit at the computers. We aren't streaming. All the cameras have been packed away; all that's left are the computers themselves.

It's been three days since I defeated the Moon Witch. Three days, and it feels like three years. I look over to Jacob, who gives me a lazy smile before going back to whatever game he's playing on his cell phone.

Three days, and everything has changed. For the better.

I'm just grateful no one was hurt. Even Claire came back. She apparently woke up in her bed Friday morning thinking it was all a bad dream. She didn't remember what happened, but she knew it was some-how my fault. As for her going missing, well—there were dozens of rumors about that, and none of them were nearly as wild as the truth.

"We could find another game," Rochelle says. "Change our names or wear masks and get a different persona or something. It doesn't have to be this . . . final."

"We need to do this," I say. "*I* need to do this."

She sighs.

"I know," she says. "It's just . . . we have such a large following now. We could stream *anything*."

"I'm not going to risk it," I say. I raise an eyebrow. "And I'm surprised you're willing to."

She shrugs. "Fame is pain. Or something."

I've had enough of fame.

The Friday after that final stream, it had been nearly impossible to get down the hall without having a dozen kids stopping me and asking whether or not any of it had been real. It was too much. At least for me. Rochelle had *loved* being the center of attention. She didn't seem to remember much of what happened, but she was totally okay hamming it up for anyone who would listen.

Even more fun, Jacob and I got detention for skipping school, and we were all grounded that night. Thankfully, Rochelle had no issue convincing my parents to let us all hang out tonight—especially once she said *why* we were all hanging out.

Like I said—those dimples. They can convince anyone, anything.

But they aren't working on me.

"Come on," I say. "The sooner we get this over with, the less chance we have of changing our minds."

"You're *sure*?" she asks. "If we do another stream, you could buy a new phone . . ."

"Rochelle . . ." Jacob intones from the sofa. "Drop it."

She glares at him.

Then she looks at me.

"Fine," she says. "But for the record, I'm willing to take the risk of being haunted by a ghost if that means fame and money."

I roll my eyes. But she doesn't press it. I know she's joking. I hope.

As one, our fingers go to the trackpad.

The pointer is already hovered over a button on our streaming account page.

> **DELETE ACCOUNT?**

We look at each other. Nod.

We delete our stream.

Later that night, I am curled up in my bed, reading an actual book. But I can't focus. I keep thinking about **DARK[room]**. About the Moon Witch.

Something about her defeat doesn't sit right. I still fully expect to see her out of the corner of my vision. I still turn on all the lights when entering a room or opening my closet. And since I still haven't gotten a new phone, there's no way to check the app to see if her name is crossed off. But I have to believe it is. We won. Just in time, we won.

"It's over," I whisper to myself. "It has to be."

After a few more minutes of staring at the same page, I sigh and close the book. I reach over to turn off the light . . .

. . . and a small red ball rolls out from under my bed, knocking into my desk.

My heart stops.

"You took my brother away," comes a small voice from under the bed. *"It's your fault, Beatrice. You took him away, and I had to find new friends to play with."*

I watch in horror as my laptop opens and turns on. As my streaming email loads.

I haven't checked the account since defeating the game.

Even from here, I can see it is filled with hundreds of new emails.

"But you helped me, Beatrice. You helped me find new friends. Now I have so many people to play with. All because of you."

The Twin's voice fades, and for a while I sit there, heart hammering in my chest, wondering if I imagined it all.

I defeated you! I . . .

But then I remember—I only captured one of the Twins in my camera. I thought that would banish both of them.

Clearly I was wrong.

The ball still sits at the base of my desk.

Minutes crawl by. Nothing else happens.

Finally, my heart still pounding, I make my way over to my desk and open the first email.

And as I read, my heart drops to my feet.

I don't know what to do. I watched your stream and took a screenshot like you asked me. And then the DARK[room] app downloaded on its own. I thought it was a promotional thing. I wanted to know if it was real or just a prank. So I started to play . . .

I stop reading and go back to the inbox.

All of the subject lines are similar.

All are begging for help.

There are over a thousand.

"*So many new friends,*" the remaining Twin whispers by my ear. I look over, but without my phone, I can't see him. But apparently, many other people can. "*We should thank you, Beatrice. We have more friends to play with than we ever could have dreamed, because of what you did. Your stream shared us with more people than we ever could have dreamed. Everyone who watched, everyone who took a picture . . . they're all playing now. All of this is possible because of you.*"

My computer pings.

Another terrified email from a fan. Another victim to **DARK[room]**'s curse.

And another.

And another . . .

ACKNOWLEDGMENTS

This may come as a surprise, but I was a complete nerd growing up.

Like the characters in this book, my friends and I spent our early high school years watching anime and reading manga, making our own costumes and going to cons (or just wandering around the neighborhood acting like fools).

And we played scary video games. Late into the night. Though I don't think we ever released any actual ghosts . . .

To that end, my first thanks goes to that original crew. Kerrie and Kayleigh, Eric and Geoff, Erin and Paula. Ben, who also helped clarify a few things about streaming. And Beatrice (no, not the character, but I appreciate you letting me use your name!) for ensuring this hit the right beats. This book would not exist without all of you, and even though we've all gone in different directions, memories of consuming too much sugar and caffeine and scaring ourselves silly playing games until three a.m. will stay with me forever.

As will the knee-jerk reaction to hum the *Doug* theme song whenever I'm scared. (Try it—it helps.)

Which reminds me—a huge thanks to my parents, for letting us have all those game nights in the first place. See? Games *were* productive uses of time!

My forever thanks to my friend and editor David Levithan, for helping bring this book to life and memorializing so many great moments in photo. Hmm . . . I should go back and make sure there aren't any ghosts in those shots.

To Jana Haussmann and the entire Scholastic team—your enthusiasm for these books has been life-changing. I owe you so much. Hopefully soon we can all take a group photo together.

And finally, thanks to you, dear reader. The last few years have been rough for all of us, but hearing from you has made the silence so much more bearable. Stay spooky. Stay weird.

I look forward to sharing many more stories with you soon.

PS I'm still a nerd. Surprise!

ABOUT THE AUTHOR

K.R. Alexander is the pseudonym for author Alex R. Kahler.

As K.R., he writes thrilling, chilling books for adventurous young readers. As Alex—his actual first name—he writes fantasy novels for adults and teens. In both cases, he loves writing fiction drawn from true life experiences.

Alex has traveled the world collecting strange and fascinating tales, from the misty moors of Scotland to the humid jungles of Hawaii. He is always on the move, as he believes there is much more to life than what meets the eye. As of this writing, Seattle is currently home.

K.R.'s other books include *The Collector, The Collected, The Fear Zone, The Fear Zone 2, The Undrowned, Vacancy, Escape,* and the books in the Scare Me series. You can contact him at cursedlibrary.com.

Read more from

K. R. Alexander...

if you dare

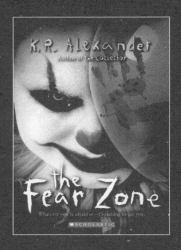

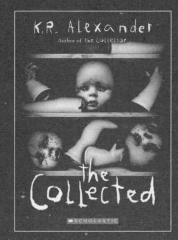